UP CLOSE AND PERSONAL

What Helen did next

JEFF LUCAS

Authentic

First published 2011 by Authentic Media Limited
Presley Way, Crownhill, Milton Keynes, MK8 0ES
www.authenticmedia.co.uk

British Library Cataloguing in Publication Data

A catalogue record for this book is available from the
British Library

ISBN-13: 978-1-85078-888-1

Cover design by Phil Houghton
Printed and bound in Great Britain by Cox and Wyman, Reading

To Chris and Jeanne; *aloha* and thanks for many
years of friendship.

Acknowledgements

Many thanks to Tamsin Kendrick, an award-winning poet and skilful writer, for the collaboration that enabled me to write again as a late twenty-something female.

And to my long-suffering and mostly smiling editor, Ali Hull, who certainly did overtime on this one.

Finally, to Mark Finnie at Authentic. The end of an era for me, Mark. All the best.

WEDNESDAY, MARCH 31st

I've decided to try again to keep a diary. What with Dad being killed – and trying to cope with that – and turning Hayley into a human being – I couldn't bring myself to write. But I read somewhere that keeping a journal can help with grief and frankly, at the moment, I am prepared to try anything. Even exorcism . . .

THURSDAY, APRIL 1st

The demons have departed, I hope. Good riddance, and don't come back.

I have been thoroughly exorcised: at least my flat has been. I mentioned to Vanessa (or V as she is in my diaries), my ever-smiling and insanely spiritual best friend, that sleep has been difficult recently. Actually, *difficult* is an understatement. I've been battling unbearable sleeplessness that has me staring wide-eyed through the shadowy gloom at the ceiling for hours at a time. I find myself wanting to take a hammer to my alarm clock, because its hands just crawl around the dial. And then, when I actually drift into a fitful catnap for more than 35 seconds, it jerks me back into consciousness with a deafening clanging that can be heard in Belgium. Come noon each day I'm exhausted. And desperate.

Enter Christian demon slayer V. She has 'discerned' that my flat has been infested by insomnia sleep-devils and she must come at once to reclaim my home as '*Shalom* territory', where *'peace is truly my portion'* and to *'re-establish the boundaries of blessing as God did with the land of Canaan.'*

My flat is a second floor paradise. It's small, kissed with Victorian charm (lots of stripped pine floorboards, high plaster ceilings and even an original working fireplace) and I absolutely love it. It's tucked in a side street off Frenton-on Sea's windy Promenade. If I stand on tiptoe I can spot the sea from my bedroom window. I do that most mornings. The IKEA Swedish kitsch clashes with the urns and blushing Victorian naked nymphs on my cream fireplace tiles, but it suits me. The burgundy emulsioned walls in my sitting-room make the place feel warm and cosy.

Back to my house 'cleansing.' V brought along her assortment of intercessory accessories. She calls it 'the basket of banishment', and it's a serious bit of kit, a vital weapon for an on-fire, warrior princess bride of Christ like her. Mind you, the princess bride part is stunningly accurate when it comes to V. She is head-turningly gorgeous, and unfailingly kind. Kindness is a helpful balancing quality for the slightly mad. She has beautiful shoulder length hair, a figure which wouldn't look out of place on a fashion catwalk in Milan, and amazing teeth. Gleaming white and perfectly straight, V's molars are a wonder to behold.

But gorgeous or not, I still had a fright when she knocked on my front door. I say knocked; she actually pounded on the door three times (with a one second pause between each thud) as if to announce to the dark spirits within that a divinely-sent bailiff had arrived to evict them.

At first, I didn't know if she was serious or if this was part of some elaborate April Fool. She was dressed all in white (symbolising unblemished purity) with white ultra skinny jeans which looked sprayed on, white *Dolce and Gabbana* sweatshirt, a white puffa jacket, even white furry earmuffs. She had slathered her perfect cheeks with olive oil. (V gets through lots of olive oil when she's banishing). Yes, she loves Jesus very much, and she is barmy. But who am I to talk? This lack of sleep has been getting me down and I'm tempted to do anything for some real rest. I'd even strip naked and sprint down the Promenade if I thought it would guarantee me a full eight hours. Hey, I'd probably do a seafront streak for six.

V decided I should also be dressed in white as a symbolic gesture of something I now can't remember. This intercessory fashion choice was a problem, because I don't have any white clothing. In the past, white has not been very flattering to my ever-so-slightly fuller figure, although these days, my clothes have been hanging off me. So with no white at hand, I had to settle for wearing a crumpled grey T-shirt and tracksuit bottoms. And I wrapped an old sheet around my middle, which made me look like an ancient Roman jogger in a toga.

The 'exorcism' itself was odd. V said we had to permeate the flat with God's music and proceeded to blast an old Amy Grant CD out on my CD player, which she carried around into each room: lounge, bedroom, kitchen, bathroom, toilet – even the airing cupboard got a brief dose of Amy and had to give up its demons, which might be a good thing because the immersion heater's been a bit iffy lately. Apparently V also wanted to bring along some lamb's blood to daub on the door frames, but good old James, her soon-to-be partner in 'God's holy plan of matrimony for the avoidance of carnality and the replenishment of the planet' (as V puts it) managed to talk her out of it. I am sooooooo looking forward to being their bridesmaid – and hope I have got over not being able to sleep by then – not much fun being exhausted. And I wish being engaged to V didn't have to mean that James and I cannot be best buddies any longer, but it does.

Anyway, back to tonight's deliverance session. We had to settle for yet more extra, extra virgin oil, rather than slaughter a lamb. V bought the oil from a stall in Frenton market. The Irish stall-owner told her it was made by Sicilian nuns who trampled the olives with their bare feet while reciting the rosary. After we took Amy on tour through the flat, V daubed virgin oil all over my door frames, liberally dabbed the headboard and foot of my bed and then completed the job by daubing the word 'rest' in oil on my forehead, which I'm sure will result in some massive spots by tomorrow morning. Then we sat down for a long time and she held my hands and prayed with me, and as crazy as she is sometimes, it was good to hear words reflecting the tenacity of her faith.

I've found it so hard to pray recently. I can't seem to summon up the energy. Her certainty was both reassuring, and disconcerting. I felt inspired, but excluded. Perhaps one day I'll be able to pray with such confidence. I wonder. I confess that, during the extended prayer, I caught myself pondering the top of V's bowed head and wondering what hair conditioner she uses. Is it one specifically for blonde hair? That's me: my friend is battling the powers of evil and I'm pondering my next trip to Boots.

Not sure why we Christians tend to think that doing spiritual warfare demands that we use Edwardian language and shout, as if Satan is a deaf character out of a costume drama.

'I command you, spirits of restlessness and anxiety, *be gone* in the *Name of Jesus*!!', V hollered. *Be gone*? All sounds a bit *Wuthering Heights* to me. 'Be removed from this place, and be bound now and cast out henceforth into the midst of the sea!'

Apparently repetition is also required, perhaps because evil spirits don't always get the message the first time. 'You have no authority here, I said you have no authority here, I said *you have no authority here*!'

That's when an eerie voice from below spoke. 'I don't have any authority here, but I am trying to watch *Coronation Street*, so can you keep it down?' It was poor old Mr Granger who lives in the ground floor flat immediately below me. He's very sweet and doesn't usually complain, but was obviously finding the banishing too loud.

V turned her attention to praying specifically for me, which involved her cooing some lovely, gentle words while giving me a good upper back massage in the process.

At last, after about an hour, she announced that the deed was done, and said we should get together for lunch tomorrow to talk. As I hugged her goodnight, I yawned, which she took as a sign of breakthrough in the heavenly realms.

Dear V. It was lovely to have her company tonight. She is a such a bustling presence, making tea, (camomile of course), tutting about the dust, lighting candles, and wafting frankincense-scented sticks around to remind us of the nativity. Am hoping that tonight I will be able to identify with the babe of Bethlehem in his swaddling clothes – and get some good sleep.

Here's to some decent swaddling. Goodnight.

FRIDAY, APRIL 2nd

Wow. Slept like a log last night, although when I first woke up I thought I had been miraculously transported into a Turkish restaurant. Perhaps V's antics did punch a hole in the heavenlies (which is one of the 11,000 things that she prayed for). Either that, or I was so exhausted by the whole intercessory process that heavenly slumber was the result. Sometimes I wish that answers to prayer came with a delivery note attached, '*This is not a coincidence or something that would have happened anyway. This is a specific answer to the prayer recently prayed, signed, God.*' The same is true when bad things happen; some of my friends at church dash to say that the devil has been at work when life turns rough. The thinking is simple. If it's good, then it's from God. If it's bad, clout the devil. Not sure it's as easy as that. Anyway, I'm grateful for the sleep, whatever its source.

Work uneventful – loads of admin. Had mid-morning coffee break with Laura (best receptionist in the Universe). Wonderful that she became – or grew into being – a Christian recently. No overnight 'Hooray I've seen the light' experience, but started coming along to our church, and has certainly got a real love for God.

'It was amazing and bizarre with it', I said, telling her about the exorcism and trying hard to enjoy sipping the horrid instant coffee that work provides, which I think is made from wood shavings.

'V was certainly thorough. Even my airing cupboard got the freedom treatment. And I did have a wonderful night's sleep – for the first time in ages. But I'm a bit worried. If God has answered V's prayers, do you think that means that he is into all the stuff that she does?'

Laura smiled. 'You do worry a lot. Surely what matters is that you got some sleep?'

'I suppose so. V is lovely but she does some odd things. I'm not sure that I want to be like that – it's just not the way I'm wired. And the little spots on my forehead this morning are proof that I can't take that much olive oil.' Laura nodded.

'We're all a bit strange, aren't we? Just because God works with us, surely it doesn't mean he endorses everything we do?'

Makes sense. She's incredibly wise, considering she's such a new Christian. That sounds patronising, but it's true. Some Christians seem to wait for years to figure out some of the things that she has discovered in a few months. Her wisdom comes liberally sprinkled with uncertainty, which is wonderful. She'll say something profound and then ask me if she got it right. Her hesitancy shows that she's trying to learn as much as she can. Of course, developing wisdom doesn't start when we choose to follow Jesus. Some of Laura's straightforward common sense is true wisdom. God didn't start working in her life when she prayed a prayer of Christian commitment. Big thought to ponder . . .

Wondered if pondering might be part of my sleep problem. I spend so much time agonising over questions that are almost impossible to answer. Perhaps even realising that is an answer to prayer? Or maybe not . . . there I go again.

Laura also impresses me because she seems so contented with her work. She looks like a high flying business executive as she sits behind our reception counter. Great hair, stylish business suits, perfect nails, she looks like she's resting for a moment on her way to the boardroom. Don't get me wrong – her role is important. As receptionist she's the face of our department in Social Services; the first point of contact for some very distressed people. She's always under incredible pressure, but manages to answer every phone call with warmth as well as efficiency. She welcomes each visitor with a smile that isn't always such a familiar sight in local government offices. It's just that she could have gone for a different career, but seems utterly happy to do what she does: meeting people.

Her one huge weakness is Dave, that awful on/off boyfriend, who apparently is very much off at the moment, thank God. Not sure if they finished because she started coming to church, or if the breakup was coincidental. Laura doesn't open up about him much, which worries me. But I do know that he's moved out, is off somewhere in Europe working (he's a bricklayer), and right now it seems there's no plans for them to get back together. From the snippets I've picked up, that sounds good.

Got together with V for lunch – her usual immaculate self. Have I chosen friends like V and Laura (both more stylish and beautiful than me) in order to punish myself?

Anyway, had light lunch in Marinabean (okay, V did light: salad. I did *almost* light: pizza with salad). We talked about last night's banishment session, and she was obviously thrilled I'd slept well, but then she popped the question I'd been expecting and dreading. 'Helen, we need to talk in order to get to the roots of this sleeplessness problem you've been having. One good night's sleep is great . . . but we both know that there are some things we need to talk through . . .'

The truth is, getting to the roots of my sleeplessness isn't rocket science; no revelation is needed there (and probably no interference from demons either). I know exactly what is causing it – but haven't wanted to admit it, either aloud or on paper. But with Dad's murder now 18 months ago – is it really? – I'm still struggling to like this town, where it all happened, and to cope with life – and to sleep.

I can't think of a better way to say this, without it sounding disrespectful to Dad – but murder is so un-Frenton. We have the occasional Saturday night drunken punch-ups, and there was a spate of burglaries last year, but Dad's death is the most dramatic criminal event that has ever happened around here. I still try to avoid the High Street whenever I can, and walk very fast indeed when I pass the spot where he died. Everything seems tinged with grey since he went, which is a tragedy in itself, because the very thought of Frenton used to mean sun and blue skies for me emotionally.

Since his death, I've found out that there's no map for grief, no prissy Sat-nav voice telling you where you are in the 'process' as some people call it. Grief isn't a process – that's far too mechanical. I'm not even sure it's a journey, because that suggests that you feel you're going somewhere, that there's some purpose or clear destination. But since he's been gone, there have been times when I feel like I'm staggering around on a chilly, fog bound moor, looking for him and knowing that he's nowhere to be found. People have told me that he's with Jesus, but I'd like him *not* to be with Jesus, but right here with me, sitting in his favourite chair, sipping a cup of tea. I don't want him off swanning around with angels; I want him listening to me with that absolute attention that no one else has ever given me.

Kristian, that obnoxious boy-band pretty worship leader at church (okay, I still haven't forgiven him for trying to snog me), tried to cheer me up by telling me that it was Dad's time. But I don't get that at all. His time? Does that mean that God operates a stopwatch, and that little children with cancer expire because, like the bloke at the dodgems on Frenton Pier, God calls 'time' and their little lives are cut short? Kristian quoted something out of the Bible – Ecclesiastes – where it says that there is a time to live and time to die, which sounds straightforward enough but then I read the rest of that book; it's the investigative journalling of a rampant hedonist who lived life so large that he makes Hugh Hefner look like a Sunday school teacher. Quotes from his meanderings should be dished out with care.

I suppose one good thing that came out of this terrible time is the *effect* that Dad's death had on Laura. She found Dad's memorial service very moving, and said it was one of the key moments on her journey into faith. As a Christian, she could see he died knowing what he was living for. Thinking of Laura, this is the point where I'm supposed to celebrate that something redemptive has come out of all this tragedy – and I *am* glad – but to be honest, given the choice between someone being helped by Dad's death and Dad not being dead, I'd choose the latter. I'm not sure I'm supposed to even say or think that. The standard thought is usually that one is glad that, whatever the cost, there is another 'soul' in the kingdom. Trouble is, Dad's in the kingdom of heaven, and I want him to be a kingdom person still here on the earth – with me.

Anyway, when V said that we needed to talk things out, she was obviously wanting to know how I was doing with the grief about Dad. She's my best friend, so we talked and cried together endlessly initially after he died – but it's been a while since we last had an in-depth conversation about it. She wanted an update, which is kind and caring, but I felt too exhausted to get into it right then, so I deflected the question, and said I was okay. And then asked if she had heard the rumour about Robert and Nola, the leaders of our lovely church.

'I've heard that they're on the move, which is awful if it's true.' V stirred her latte, nodded grimly but said nothing, as if she was waiting for a message from the Lord that would confirm or deny the rumour. Her furrowed brow indicated deep concentration.

Thank God for Robert and Nola – they're wise, kind, and generally fabulous. Robert's listening skills are not as honed as Dad's, but he comes a very close second. What is so helpful is what they *don't* say. I blab on and cry and rant and tell them how utterly angry I am at God and they don't try to fix me; in fact they don't try to do anything other than be there. One of the problems about being a Christian is that there are so many people who are keen to sort you out, give their opinion, or even make statements that are allegedly from God. Obviously V does this to me all the time, but I can handle it because I know that she loves me so much and means well. But Robert and Nola don't try to rush me into 'growth' or 'progress.' It's like they walk with me. Actually, much of the time they stand still with me.

I don't know what I would have done without them: Mum has been wonderful, and her new found faith seems to be helping her, but I don't want to dump all my stuff on her – she's got enough of her own pain without me adding to it. But if Robert and Nola are leaving Frenton and taking up a ministry appointment somewhere else, that is *not* the will of God.

And even if it is, it's not the will of me.

We still need them. The church isn't over the crisis caused by the Hemmings leaving, although it has been much better since they took their hyper-critical sniping off to upset a different set of people. Their power trip at New Wave Christian Fellowship lasted a long time, and you don't get over that immediately. Robert had the courage to take them on – suppose someone new didn't have, and they came back? Although I guess, since Mrs

Hemming got slapped round the face by Mum at Dad's funeral, they would probably be too embarrassed to return to the scene of that encounter.

Although they have left the church, they have not left the area, and I gather they have been spreading rumours about NWCF. Not sure where they are going now – I've heard that they meet with a few other people in their home – perhaps folks who are as spiritually deep (and lethal) as they are. Sorry. Shouldn't have written that. In criticising them for being vicious, I'm being vicious. Weird how we can end up displaying the character traits that we so dislike in others.

Anyway, the blank look on V's beautiful face showed me that word of Robert and Nola's leaving hadn't yet reached her, either from humans or God himself. Perhaps it's not true after all, in which case, hooray. Undeterred by my deflection, V pressed in: 'So, Helen, how are things with you . . . you know, with your dad . . .' I stared into my coffee as if there was something fascinating lurking in the froth, and I wanted to say, that's the problem – I'm *not with* my dad. And that means that everything is still depressing.

Work has been okay. The time off I had after Dad died didn't do me any good at all, even though it was good of them to give it to me – compassionate leave – I suppose it was the least they could do. But all I did was sit around my flat, doing nothing. Yes, I was glad not to have to be a social worker for a while (people would tell me their stuff and all I wanted to do was to scream *'You think you've got problems? Try this one – my dad was stabbed to death!'*) but I didn't know what to do with the time.

V told me that this would be a good opportunity to 'dig a deeper well with the Lord', but I didn't have a spade, and I already have running water. I didn't feel like doing anything that involved intensity or effort, and found myself wandering down to Frenton Pier and plying the slots with twenty pences, and then getting irritated for feeling bad about gambling. I wasn't exactly living it large in Las Vegas, and I don't think God was bothered. The apocalypse isn't likely to be launched because I lost 40 pence on the pier. At least I hope not. Actually, I lost about £3.60.

I got exhausted by the idea that I'm supposed to be processing something. For at least a year, there was a black hole inside me – how was I to navigate through that? Although it's better now, it has been replaced by a slightly hollow feeling. I want to think about Dad, but not feel the pain. It's easier to not go there – it always ends up with the same result: grief.

And Aaron is useless. I can't even define what he is – a vaguely boyfriendish boyfriend? Just a friend? Whatever. Even when he does come round – which has happened a few times – the place seems emptier than normal. My even being with him at all has been a surprise. Since Dad was stabbed (it hurts even to write that) when trying to rescue Aaron from that gang of kids, I found it easy for a while to hate Aaron as well. My reasoning was simple: if Aaron hadn't been on the High

Street that night, then there would have been no trigger to the events that followed. And of course, that is true. But the truth of it doesn't make Aaron guilty of anything, and although it's taken me a while to see that, I've made a start on stopping blaming him, if that makes sense. He still feels guilty, of course, but he doesn't know what to say.

So he mooches around the flat and plays me tracks from his iPod; songs about love, guilt, faithful friendship – he says that the songs can say what he can't. Mostly they make me cry. Just about any music still does. Even the advert for toilet paper with the puppy reduced me into a heap in the terrible few months after Dad went. As for Aaron, I can't figure out whether he likes or loves me, or feels sorry for me, and however many tracks he plays, I can't get our relationship clear in my head. So having him around seems to create a confusing vacuum. And I don't have the first clue what I feel about him.

The case itself remains unsolved. The police have drawn a complete blank; there were no witnesses, and the only one on the scene was Aaron. He says that what with it being so dark, and the kids wearing hoodies, he hadn't a clue who they were or what they looked like. I wish the police could make some progress though – and I hope that they haven't given up. There's something about knowing that my dad's killer is still out there that makes me feel that he's not at rest.

Where was I? Oh yes, going back to work . . . after a week or two of tearful shuffling around doing nothing useful I went back to work. And there I found, not so much a ray of sunshine, but maybe the vaguest hint of it. Social work can be scary, painful, deeply challenging and occasionally a little bit wonderful. Hayley, one of the long term 'cases' that I've been handling, seems to be becoming nicer (although only slightly) – and – believe it or not – show a bit of interest in God. She came along to Dad's memorial service, and stunned me with a smile. Since then she's been slightly easier to deal with, which is amazing, considering her history. She was removed from her dysfunctional parental home because of the alcohol, drug abuse and occasional domestic violence – her parents seemed to think that Saturday night literally was alright for fighting, and therefore did so – in front of the children. In the end, Hayley's aunt (Mrs Tennant) offered to look after her, and while she is not the brightest spark in the world, (and has complete disdain for social workers, especially ones named Helen), she has at least provided Hayley with some stability while keeping her in the orbit of her wider family. I keep an eye on things because Mrs T is fostering, not adopting Hayley. Call me cynical, but fostering means financial help, and adopting doesn't. But it's better because I get to monitor the situation with occasional home visits. Hayley is seventeen, so in a year will be making her own choices about where she'll live.

Speaking of work, I've a got a new supervisor, a senior social worker called Maeve. She's rather strange – the best way to describe her is *grey*. I don't know how old she is – she could be thirty, but she's so thin, she looks fifty. Her faced is lined and the lines fall most naturally into a vague frown. She rarely smiles, and everything about her is drab. She was transferred into our department from another borough. I don't know if she's married (there's no rings on her bony fingers), and she's not the kind of person to have anything nearing a personal conversation with. I've tried. Conversation with her is strictly about work. She seems preoccupied with systems and procedures, and gets tetchy if our paperwork isn't completely up to date. Our weekly team meetings – all six of us together, chaired by Maeve – tend to meander, but with little warmth and small talk. She speaks very quickly, and whenever I talk to her, she punctuates what I say by nodding like one of those dogs that sit on the back shelves of cars. She says, 'Sure, sure', which seems like code for 'Shut up, shut up now.'

Speaking of small talk, that's what I did when V pressed me about my dad.

'I'm doing fine with it at the moment V. It's never going to be okay, is it?'

V opened her mouth to speak, and for a terrible moment I thought she was going to launch into a little speech about how one day the angels will sing, the trumpet will sound, and everything will be okay, and that we all need to learn to live in the light of eternity. I think I silenced her with an alarmed look. Dear V. At least she knows when to stop. Mostly. And she does mean well.

Enough for now. I need to have another crack at getting to sleep. I know V's probably going to ask me for a 'praise report' next time I see her (because she does love me), and if I have to concede the 'failure' of sleeplessness, she'll be hot footing around the flat again in her role as an amateur witch-finder general, and probably tell me that she has discerned that my sleep problem is due to a young Christian virgin being sacrificed around these parts. Speaking of Christian virgins, that would be me, still. Too tired to get into that now. Can't stop yawning. Maybe the exorcism is working.

SATURDAY, APRIL 3rd

Slept until noon. Hallelujah, and praise be. Think maybe V should launch a new sleep ministry, perhaps in partnership with a bedding company. Only outdoor event today was a walk on the Prom, spoiled by a low flying seagull that managed to decorate my head. Yuk.

Bumped into James jogging along the Prom. He's so excited about finding V as the love of his life, and ecstatic about the wedding. As we nattered about the arrangements, I found myself wondering – is James a little boring (as I've always thought, which was why I was afraid of ending up with him) or is it that his life had become boring, and now that he has V, he's become a more interesting, alive person? Delighted for them both, but am concerned to admit that I thought that James was looking fine in his running gear . . . Argh – do I fancy him, now he's not available? I spend half my life trying to avoid getting involved with him, and when he's on the verge of marrying my best friend, I start to think he's hot. *What am I thinking*? Naughty girl,

Helen. Stop that right now. Black Lycra is good on him though.

Later

Can't sleep. Middle of the night, so can't call V. Think that my sleep problems may be due to the ridiculously long lie-in that I had today rather than the fruit of concerted demonic attack. Or maybe the mild distraction of surprisingly hunky looking James in Lycra. Is he getting better looking?

SUNDAY, APRIL 4th

Finally got to sleep at 5am and then slept through my alarm clock, so I skipped church this morning; didn't have the heart for it anyway, to be honest. I haven't been very good at going recently, it all seems like so much effort. This afternoon I got a phone call from Robert and Nola, thought at first they were calling to send me on a guilt trip, (which is unlike them, but don't accuse me of being logical), but they wanted to explain that Robert has decided to resign his position as leader of NWCF and they are planning to move up north. So the rumours are true. Fine. I guess they can leave. Everybody else does.

I don't mean that. I don't know what we're going to do without them. They have been such a calming presence in our little community, and a bedrock of support for me. I've said it before, but they are such wonderful listeners, and don't try to fix me. And I love their hugs.

Ever since the phone call I've had a horrible feeling in my stomach, like the black hole within has come back and expanded. I wanted to say that maybe I'd leave the church too (which I wouldn't, but it feels like a good response to their going), but then Robert shocked me by asking if I would be part of the search committee that coordinates the hunt for a new church leader. Apparently the actual selection is done by the congregation taking a vote (which sounds like a beauty contest with a Bible), but Robert said that my common sense attitude and my experience with people as a social worker would be helpful in finding and they seem very keen, and although I'm angry that they are deserting me (okay, leaving), perhaps it's one thing that I can do in return for all their hours of listening.

I did get another visit from V tonight. She brought a little bottle of oil, for an exorcism top-up, in case the first one hadn't stuck. She also brought a photo of the most beautiful bridesmaid's dress I have ever seen, which I am to wear for the wedding. I'm so relieved. I have been a tiny bit worried that she might choose something odd, although her fashion sense is always great, helped by the fact that she'd look fabulous in a bin bag. But I shouldn't have been. The dress is a stunning blue, which will match my rather lovely blue eyes: my best feature, even though I say so myself.

At this talk of weddings prompts another worry: I don't think I'm so interested in marriage any more. I'm not totally off men, as my rather strange relationship with Aaron proves – and my momentary checking out of

James. I remember when it was pretty much all I thought about . . . the whole romance schbang, the wedding, and the naughty bits . . .

Right now, I don't have the energy. Perhaps that's why I'm okay with the vague boyfriend that I have in Aaron. Yes, he is weird and I cannot get my head round him being a raving zealot in college and now being an often drunk, very ex-committed Christian. He seems willing to believe any old bizarre idea, and thinks that flitting from notion to notion is a sign of bohemian sophistication. His job at that secondhand bookshop doesn't help – he seems to grab hold of whatever idea he's currently reading about, and as things are always slow there, he reads a lot. Perhaps too much for his own good.

But I think that his company suits me (some of the time) because he makes no demands. He comes over and broods in my flat, plays me songs, drinks red wine from the bottle and stares at the wall. But I always feel that little bit emptier after he's gone. Sometimes we kiss. Sometimes we don't. Sometimes I care and sometimes I don't. Caring seems like far too much effort. Talking of effort, I have a case-visit tomorrow morning, with Hayley.

Been thinking about my poor attendance record at church lately. I've found myself becoming far more critical when I do go there, than I used to be. Instead of entering in to all that's going on, I've become a spectator. I find myself fixating on irritating people during the worship, and things that didn't bother me before now drive me nuts. Like the flag wavers, for example. Having a supply of flags at the front, that anyone can go and use in sung worship, was probably a great idea once – colourful, creative, another expression of praise, blah blah. And okay, some people dance with them well . . . and maybe the colours do have some symbolic meaning – although who decides? But now I groan when someone makes the move towards them.

I think I stopped taking them seriously a few months ago when Kristian dramatically removed his guitar while leading worship, whispered 'I have to do this right now' breathlessly into the microphone, and then marched over, picked up a red flag and started twirling with it. Unfortunately he got into it, and within seconds was leaping around like mad, thrusting and lunging with the flag, which caused huge consternation on the front row. Kristian wanted to worship the Lord without inhibition, and they wanted to keep their eyesight intact. The best bit was when he got too keen, enfolded himself in the canvas, and tottered across the platform. When he finally crashed to the floor, a minor expletive was heard from within the furls of the flag. He escaped with a minor cut to the head.

Ever since then, the flags have done nothing for me. Little Doris obviously saw some flag waving at a conference, and now she stands at the front, waggling a flag from side to side like a windscreen wiper. The move is the same for the fast songs as the slow, and the waving doesn't even match the beat. What do visitors think? Is she signalling a distant plane to land, or perhaps heralding the departure of a train?

I've decided that having critical faculties is obviously good – we don't need to kiss our brains goodbye – but mine are currently driven by pain, and grief. I've caught myself going to church looking for things to be upset about, and church being what it is (crammed with fallen human beings like me) there's no shortage of things that will do. The trouble is, being irritated is a habit – maybe even an addiction, and it's hard to break out of it. So I find myself making excuses for not going to church at all. Not good. Am worried that my hyper-critical attitude might be very unhelpful in my role on the search committee. How am I supposed to be of any use if I spend most of my time seething, when I actually am in church?

Before V left, she asked me if I had any sin that I should confess. Apparently my transgressions might contribute to my sleeplessness. The words 'Lycra' and 'James' came to mind, but I decided not to mention them. We talked about my critical attitude for a while.

Oh, and she gave me an envelope that Nola sent over. It contained a kind little note (Nola's good at those) and a leaflet about grief counselling. Apparently, during the week our church hall is rented out to different groups, from new mums' exercise classes to AA meetings. A new group is meeting weekly for a group counselling session for people who have lost loved ones. Nola asked if I might like to give it a try?

Am not sure. I've never been one for group sobbing sessions, despite all these years in an evangelical charismatic church. I guess I am struggling to get over what happened to my father, so it might help. V has suggested a couple of Christian counsellors I could go to, but I've had more than my fair share of being prayed over and prayed for. I manage to fake a weak smile and tell them I feel much better thank you very much, but mostly it's for their benefit. Inside, nothing changes. Perhaps I need some therapy that is accredited, someone who is qualified to get me through this? Don't know if this group will fit that bill or if it's a bunch of amateurs. But perhaps they'll have some answers for me.

I feel bad writing this, but sometimes I think the church is so far removed from the rest of the world that it ignores the good that can come out of it. We're all human after all and just because someone isn't a Christian doesn't mean that they don't have anything useful to give. Do Christians have the monopoly on the truth? I look around and see people getting on fine without God and religion. They're out and about living happy healthy lives, whereas I look around at the Christians I know and see them struggling with all sorts of things. Christianity seems to be making their lives even more complicated, not better. Maybe I'll try and do what any normal person would do in my situation, get some proper, university educated psychological help. What harm could it possibly do? Mmm. Am I saying that Christians aren't normal? Silly generalisation really. Although some certainly aren't.

Anyway, after V had gone, I had a natter on the phone with Mum about nothing in particular. It doesn't seem to matter that our conversations are often about trivia:

we've become closer since Dad died, and I'm amazed at her strength. Told her about the grief counselling; she said she thought it could be a good idea. Asked her if she'd like to join me, but she said that might be inhibiting for me, and that perhaps this should be something for me to do. Typical of her, putting me first.

MONDAY, APRIL 5th

Good sleep last night, apparently unaffected by my sins. Case visit with Hayley today. Mrs Tennant, Hayley's aunt, with the forever-present Mayfair ciggie attached to her lip, was her usual self. 'The duffle coat is 'ere', she announced as she opened the door. I always take a deep breath before stepping into the nicotine aura that fills Mrs Tennant's house; but as I walked into the smoggy living room, Hayley did something that seriously cheered me up. She jumped up and gave me a hug. This is a step forward, and when you consider the cold hearted cow that she used to be, the change in her is gradual but remarkable. We chatted for a while about the new hairdressing course she's doing at the community college. A few months ago I wouldn't have wanted to see her anywhere near anybody while armed with a pair of scissors, but there's a definite softness about her now – well, a hint of it anyway. She chatted on, and Mrs Tennant sat and wheezed quietly, her cigarette ash growing to an impossible length. At one point I think that Mrs Tennant fell completely asleep, while miraculously still smoking her cigarette.

And then came the moment that brought Mrs Tennant very much back to life – with a bang. Hayley asked if she could come to church with me next Sunday. Mrs Tennant spluttered and swore. 'Don't you get tied up with all that litigious stuff . . . it'll do yer 'ead in, my girl.' I tried to gently explain that the word Mrs Tennant was looking for was in fact 'religious', but by now, she was in full flow. 'My father got himself into God, and he was never the same again. He went barmy. Used to have loads of fun before he got God, or God got 'im. Became a pro-phylactic Jew. Got circumcised when he was 53 and grew his hair into ringlets. Mad as a 'atter. Stay away, my girl, stay away.'

I so wanted to let Mrs Tennant know that a prophylactic was a condom and that proselytised should be her word of choice, but there was no point. I let her blether on, how the old man left the little bit of money he had to the local synagogue and how that's all those church people want anyway, yer hard earned cash, and it's all brain-washing, people kiddin' themselves that there's some meaning to life when life is a messy hell and then you die and . . .

. . . and as she droned on, for a moment I wondered if she might be right. Actually, it lasted more than a moment. What if there was no God, no power anywhere to stop a bunch of thugs from putting a knife in my Dad's heart, and if all of our singing was serenading the ceiling and kidding ourselves that there was love in a loveless Universe? That's what I hate about doubt. It doesn't call ahead, and make an appointment, but mugs us when we're least expecting it. Here I was, supposed to be glad that Hayley was coming to church, and the irrational ranting of old Mrs Tennant was turning me into a potential member of the Humanist Society. Anyway, I mumbled something about picking Hayley up at 9.30am on Sunday and stumbled out, gripped by my usual default condition: confusion.

Phoned V and told her about it, and she said that doubt was normal and that she'd doubted her faith once, years ago, which didn't help, because it sounded like her faith wobble was ancient history. Also unhelpful was her asking again if I had unconfessed sin in my life that might be the root of both sleeplessness and doubt. Wondered if James had spotted my little Lycra-fuelled glance, and had told V about it. No, it was only for a second.

Aaron came round tonight and insisted on reading some Nietzsche to me. What a happy tonic. Not.

TUESDAY, APRIL 6th

Loads of admin at work today, not my favourite thing, followed by a conversation about Hayley and then a crisis.

Had a chat with Maeve, about taking Hayley to church. Actually, not so much a chat – more like a mini-lecture. She said it could create a few problems if Hayley decided to stay in the church, with me being her social worker. I suppose we'll sort that out when the time comes. I started to give Maeve an overview of Hayley's case history, but she cut me off before I was even three sentences in.

'Sure, sure, I know Hayley's background, thank you. I've reviewed every case file that is being handled by each of the six members of my team. What's the presenting issue, please? Fill me in.' Maeve has this nasal monotone that makes me want to scream. Not only that, but as she interrupted me I found myself wondering why she wears such creased jumpers. There's clothing that isn't ironed and is fashionably crumpled, like stuff from *Abercrombie and Fitch*, which produces uber-grunge – and there's un-ironed. But why does Maeve look creased and yet uncool with it? This is one of the great mysteries of life.

I explained to her that Hayley has been asking me to take her to church. When I mentioned the word 'church' she wrinkled her slightly hairy upper lip in what seemed like disdain, as if church attendance was only for those who had had a full frontal lobotomy.

'If that's what your client wants, Helen, I suppose it's fine, as long as going there won't cause her upset.'

Church cause her upset? She made it sound like a very dodgy curry.

She continued, 'I suppose it's possible she might be looking for a crutch, something to get her through. People do that, don't they, when they don't feel strong enough to tackle life on their own?'

The inference was obvious. Maeve was implying, without a shred of subtlety, that everybody who has faith is weak – including me. I decided not to retaliate. Her burgeoning unwanted hair problem on her upper lip was punishment enough.

'Just be careful. Please log an appropriate notation in Hayley's file, and keep the situation under review. As long as she is clearly saying that she wants to go to church without any invitation or pressure from you, it should be fine to take her along, once or twice. If church-going becomes her permanent habit, then you need to either point her to another local congregation, or have someone else be her point of contact at your church. Is there anything else?'

I desperately wanted to tell her that there *were* a few other vital issues we should discuss: she needed to restyle her hair, buy some conditioner and pull up her saggy tights. Oh, and plug her iron in, or even buy one, and maybe even invest in an epilator – or electrolysis.

I didn't.

So Hayley can come along to NWCF, and it's fine, unless she decides to come a lot. To be very honest, that's unlikely, oh me of little faith.

After my 'lovely' chat with Maeve I ended up over at the hospital, called in by a casualty doctor who was concerned about some bruises on a baby brought in with a high temperature. These cases are so difficult, when it's my job to be suspicious. Asked for an assessment. The baby is being kept in overnight so I can check on things tomorrow when I get to speak to the paediatrician.

Mum phoned tonight and mentioned that the youth club is going well, which is good – even though I don't go there right now. I know we got what we wanted, after Dad died – we got the community centre he had been fighting for. Yes, it was renamed the Peter Sloane Centre, yes, it was launched in earnest, with me running it, and yes, he fought tooth and nail to get it, and it was a wonderful achievement, blah blah blah, get the kids off the streets, give them somewhere to go . . .

. . . and I don't give a monkey's. Not now.

Maybe it is too soon to go back there, maybe I will change my mind. I know what people expect of me as a Christian. They want me to go back to the youth club, even though I know that there is a slight possibility that my father's killers might one day walk through the door. They expect me (because this is the Christian thing), not only to forgive his murderers but to put myself smack bang in the midst of them. How am I supposed to run a youth group when the thought of a group of kids hanging out on the corner fills me with hate and fear? It's hard enough dealing with some of the kids that I encounter through work. When I started up the club, I was so full of hope for these teenagers, I believed deep down that they were good people, even though some of them had been given a bad start in life.

Now I've experienced first hand what they're capable of, in my head they are no longer vulnerable children who need loving and protecting. They are unpredictable predators. I struggle to even see them as individuals any more, just a pack of animals, laughing at people who try to be kind to them.

Luckily my mother seems to be a better (or at least stronger) person than me. She has taken over running the weekly sessions at the club, helped by church volunteers. She doesn't seem to care that she might be giving sanctuary to her husband's murderer. Or maybe she has a more simple approach, and wants to fill her empty days by doing something useful at the youth centre that's named in her husband's honour.

Love is so exhausting; to forgive and love so many people – it's too much for me. Again, my mother seems to be doing so well. She turns up at the club every week in her dangly Indian earrings (bought from Frenton market), rolls up her sleeves and gets on with it. When I asked her how she could do it, she didn't seem that fussed.

'Well, darling' she replied, 'Your dad was so passionate about that club, wasn't he? I think it's what he would have wanted. He was such a good man. It's for him.' All so beautifully logical and true, and all so very beyond me. Dad *was* a good man, which is exactly why I can't bear to even walk past the place he and I managed to put together. It all took such a lot of hard work and heartache. There aren't many truly kind and good men in the world any more and my father was one of them.

Apparently my mother has got some of the kids in the club into a new fangled meditation technique. When I inquired whether it was kosher, she replied that she found out about it from a small community of Christians called the Anamchara community, which means something like soul-friend. She gets all the youth to sit in a big circle, cross-legged, they close their eyes, sit in silence and try to imagine God. She said that some of them never experience true silence, what with their headphones plugged in all the time, computer games, televisions and parents screaming at one another. Apparently the number of fights has decreased since they began doing it. Maybe I should try it? Hope my mum and V never become close. The world couldn't cope.

Lord, please help me to even want to forgive, so I can continue what I started. Please let me start seeing these kids as human. Please give me the grace to even want to begin that journey. Amen.

Aaron texted and asked if I was interested in another session of Nietzsche. Tempt me not.

WEDNESDAY, APRIL 7th

Follow up visit on the bruised baby. The mother said that the baby slammed its arm into the side of the cot while sleeping. The paediatrician said that what she found was consistent with the mother's claim, and there's no record of any previous issues, so am happy to leave things as they are for now.

Since last night's phone call I've been thinking more about my mum, the fabulous Kitty. In the eighteen months since Dad died, she has been amazing. Perhaps that's the side that she shows me; one of the challenges about grieving around those you love most is that you don't want to make things worse for them. So you end up not fully sharing your pain with anyone at all, because it doesn't work so well with unaffected strangers. My mum has been scatty through the years, but she's always been dependable as a mum.

Odd thought: I wonder if she will ever remarry? Certainly she's attractive enough (she wears skinny jeans that I still can't even think about wearing, despite my weight loss) and she's got great skin and a gorgeous smile. I'd like to ask her about it, ask if she ever feels like she wants someone else to be there. To be honest, I don't know how I'd feel if she met someone.

Went for a wander along the Prom with Aaron tonight, which was boring. He seemed to be in a faraway place, and didn't say much. Didn't even bring Nietzsche along, thankfully. Just gazed longingly at the sea for most of the time. Turned down a chance for a Chinese with Laura in favour of the seafront walk, so was annoyed.

Am going to try the grief counselling at the church hall tomorrow night. Fingers crossed (if Christians are allowed to cross their fingers . . .).

V texted to say that she went on a 'solitary prayer walk' around Frenton earlier this evening. (I assume

this means she couldn't get anyone to go with her).
Wondered why she hadn't asked me to go along? Am
still worried that James noticed my admiring glance
the other day and has told her. Or maybe God noticed
my sideways glance and has told V who has told
James. Either way, this would not be good. Will make
sure that I look straight into James's eyes next time I
see him.

THURSDAY, APRIL 8th

Just got back from my first group grief counselling session. Learned that whereas Christianity may or may not
have the monopoly on truth, it certainly doesn't have
the monopoly on weirdness. Which was reassuring, as
I occasionally have this niggling thought that NWCF is
some sort of cult. The truth is that people, whatever
their religion, are weird, it's the human condition. We
began with that classic trust game, to bond, unify and
strengthen the group, where you have to fall backwards
into the arms of your partner. This would have been
fine apart from the fact that old Gerald, my partner, was
a very sweet man in his early eighties who had recently lost his wife to cancer. He looked like a gust of wind
would fell him, not to mention a few stone of pure
womanhood (that would be me) dropping into his
arms. The group leader took one look at us and mumbled something along the lines of 'Why don't we hold
hands and quietly look into each other's eyes instead?'
So we did.

It was horrendous.

I get freaked out when I accidentally meet someone's eye on the bus, not to mention having to stare into the eyes of a stranger for a good minute. Sixty seconds doesn't sound very long, but trust me, I swear civilisations rose and fell in the time I stared into poor Gerald's watery eyes. But it got me thinking; I can't remember the last time I looked into someone's eyes. Isn't it funny how such a simple thing, making eye contact with someone, can be so powerful? And why does it embarrass us when we accidentally do it? I guess it's intimate, like walking in on someone in the shower. Now I was starting to imagine wrinkly Gerald in the shower . . . I have to stop thinking in pictures.

The rest of the session wasn't too bad; mostly it was introducing ourselves and sharing why we had decided to come along to the group. My dad's murder was a big deal in this small town, so that made me into a minor celebrity, which I felt bad about. I didn't want to hog all the attention. I got lots of sympathetic head nodding and a middle-aged lady even got tearful when I told everyone who I was. Decided that I will go again, but haven't committed myself for the whole course yet.

FRIDAY, APRIL 8th

Went for coffee with Nola after work today. She tried to explain why she and Robert feel it's time to move north. I wanted to be understanding, but deep down I feel I've been betrayed. They have been such a big influence in my life and now they're moving away. Nola was saying how she felt God had called them to move on, and that I shouldn't worry about NWCF, as they didn't make it what it was; it's the congregation that makes a church, not its leaders. Even if she's right, I feel they have had a lot of influence when it came to smoothing over the lumps and bumps of church life. When I asked her if she was sure God was calling them up north, she laughed and said, 'Not completely, but we have put a lot of time and prayer into the decision and feel like we're making the right one. I will miss you terribly, Helen, but we can talk on the phone, and we'll come back and visit. You can even come and visit us up north. I'm sure we'll need a spare pair of hands! It's not like we're moving to Timbuktu!'

I reluctantly agreed, I suppose the world doesn't revolve around me, much as I'd like it to. It's still sad to see such good friends go though.

I love them and I'm angry with them both because I love them so much. I don't like this business of leaders 'moving on' to other church situations. I wonder how the disciples felt when Jesus said that he was going away? My memory is that they put up a fight, especially Peter. I can't say I blame them. Would love to beg Nola and Robert to stay, and then hear them say that I have changed their minds, and that everything is going to stay the same after all. Don't like change. Everything changes. Wish I could freeze the frame of life today. Scratch that. Wish I could freeze the frame of life eighteen months ago.

Tomorrow night is V's hen-party, which is odd, because it's weeks before the wedding, but she insists that it happens well in advance so that she can have a 'forty-day season of focused preparation' before the big day. When I said this sounded a bit intense, she said that in Old Testament times women were known to pamper themselves with exotic oils and spices for a whole year prior to a wedding. I'm not sure if this is what she is thinking of doing. If so, perhaps I should buy shares in Body Shop.

SATURDAY, APRIL 10th

Hen night tonight. Squeezed a year of pampering (okay, I'm not the bride, and this is not the wedding, but those are details) into a couple of hours. Have decided to make a dash for town to buy a new dress for tonight. No time to write more.

SUNDAY, APRIL 11th

Last night was the epic hen-party. I decided that my appearance did need some serious work, so I stopped off at Boots on the way home from dress shopping and bought most of the store. I'm a sucker for anything that promises to transform me into Angelina Jolie. I'd even settle for Jennifer Aniston. I spent the whole afternoon putting my hair in rollers, giving myself manicures, pedicures, I had to re-do them a couple of times due to my complete inability to keep a steady hand whilst holding a nail varnish brush. I shaved my legs, put special goo in my hair to make it soft and silky and put enough make-up on to appear in the stage show of *Cabaret*. Then I took the make-up off and reapplied it so I didn't look like I'd got two black eyes and bleeding lips. I knew it was bad when I thought that a raccoon was staring back at me from the mirror.

Finally, I put on my new dress, that I had to buy for unexpected weight loss reasons. Have to admit that, for the first time in months, I felt good about myself. There was something therapeutic about pampering and preening, it was therapy for the soul. My new dress is salmon pink with red flowers all over. Sounds hideous, but looks way better than it sounds. Decided against black. Black is flattering but too like mourning, and I didn't want to make things more difficult for myself than they already are. It seems everything still reminds me of Dad and his death: the colour black, the flowers planted by the council outside the flat, even the sound of the sea. It's funny (funny odd not funny ha-ha) because even though everywhere I go reminds me of him, I've taken down all the photos I had of him in my flat and have hidden them in a shoebox beneath my bed. They're too painful to look at. I hated doing it, in some strange way I feel like I'm contributing to his absence, but that's better than crying every time I catch a glimpse of his kind face peering out from a photo frame.

Anyway, back to the Hen. These parties are stressful as it is, but this wasn't anybody's hen-party. This was V's. There were only six of us: V, Laura, me, and three girls from the church that V used to go to. Nola was invited but couldn't come as she and Robert were out speaking somewhere.

Laura and I were supposed to be organising the hen 'games' though, as it turned out, V had a few ideas of her own. I turned up, feeling pleased with myself after all that preening. But, despite all that hard work, I was immediately upstaged by V, who was wearing a nun's outfit. Yes. A full on, black and white habit and wimple nun's outfit. It wasn't even a joke. Apparently it was to symbolise her previous devotion to being a wife of Christ and at the end of the evening she was going to remove it as a symbolic gesture representing her new life to come as a married woman. Apparently James was going to turn up and do it for her.

'So James is going to show up later and take your dress off?' giggled Laura.

V's response showed that she considered her behaviour to be entirely sane. 'Yes. This is a symbolic act of the new life that we'll embrace together', she said – going slightly pink. 'I have leggings and a T-shirt on underneath with a picture of a tiger on it. That's to represent the formidable and mysterious powers of my femininity.'

I think that might have been the last coherent thing I heard her say, not that she is coherent at the best of times. Laura had decided that even though V had ordered a lemonade when she entered the bar, she was going to have a good old Frenton hen-party, which usually involves more than a dab of alcohol. Laura did of course buy her a lemonade, she just forgot to mention the double measure of vodka she got the barmaid to put in it. I'm not suggesting that spiking drinks is ever a good idea, but the results with V were hilarious. After a couple of these, her habit was wonky, her hair was poking out all over the place and she had started to hop around to a Britney Spears song.

Just as V had her basket of banishment, Laura had her hen-bag of bawdy. After a few drinks in the pub we all returned to V's windchime-packed and incense-reeking flat and started the serious party. Laura produced a naughty hat for V to wear, that she claimed was modelled on the Tower of Babel. Mmm, not so sure about that.

Played a few silly games and then we got around to talking about men, and they got frustrated with me because I wouldn't tell them if Aaron was my full-on boyfriend or not. It was embarrassing; I feel almost ashamed of Aaron. I realised that I want to keep our relationship secret.

How can I be in a relationship with someone I am ashamed of, if you could call staring at walls, walking wordlessly (and sullenly) down the Prom, and being depressed together a relationship? Decided I must sort things out with him. We should at least have some sort of conversation about what's going on with us. The thing is, he doesn't seem to care. Not that he doesn't care about me. He makes that abundantly clear, but he doesn't like defining things, he's too scared of becoming a cliché.

Anyway, at the end of the evening James walked in, (looking very handsome), V was in the middle of one of

Laura's symbolic acts which involved her making up a song about her wedding night, with her nun's habit half off her head and the questionable Tower of Babel on her head, leaning more like the Tower of Pisa. James asked V whether it was time to take her dress off yet. We all collapsed, leaving James red-faced. Thankfully the dress stayed on. It was the best fun I've had in ages.

Have resolved to speak to Aaron soon.

Did manage to drag myself to church this morning, but spent most of my time praying that no one would head for the flags. No one did.

TUESDAY, APRIL 13th

Flurry of home visits at work today. So many dysfunctional situations, it's overwhelming.

Met Aaron after work and he was the opposite of the sullen soul that he's been for weeks. Tried to find out why he's so excited, but he said that he's on the edge of a discovery that he can't tell me about yet, but will in time. Probably discovered some weird new religious or philosophical idea which will provide him with a eureka period for a week or two. Didn't get round to talking about us. Must do. Having another go at the grief counselling group tomorrow night.

I have spent the evening screaming out at the sea, followed by a time of community singing. At the group counselling session tonight, instead of all sitting in a circle like in an AA meeting, the group leader, Anita, decided that expressing our rage was a crucial step in the grief process (there's that word again – process. Don't like it at all. Cheese is processed. Sausages are processed. People are not). Anyway, Anita, who trained in grief counselling after losing her daughter ten years ago, said she is still angry about what happened to her child, and shouting to the sea had helped her.

So we all put on our coats and made the short walk to the shore to tell the sea exactly what we thought of it. Although the group is non-religious, I couldn't help but think that this was a substitute to yelling at God, which meant I couldn't commit as well as the others. Are you allowed to shout at God? Isn't it blasphemous? Then I thought of Jesus on the cross shouting, 'My God, my God, why have you forsaken me?' and concluded that if Christ could do it, I could too.

I don't know what passing pedestrians must have thought we were doing, lining up on the sea front and shouting at the top of our lungs. I struggled to find something to say and was distracted as I was standing a metre away from Anita, who was screaming some obscenities at the horizon. Gerald was also mustering some colourful language, which shocked me; I didn't realise old people knew the words he was spurting. I managed to yell, somewhat half-heartedly, 'why me?', a few times, which frankly felt insipid and silly, and then called it a day, I think this is something I have to do in private, without a group of spectators standing on the Prom.

Afterwards we all went for a drink, where we eyed each other over our glasses. Gerald got tipsy, and started singing old Irish folk songs. At first it was almost as embarrassing as screaming at the sea, but after a while I stopped being uptight and started enjoying it for what it was. Anita acted as group choir mistress and got us all joining in on the choruses. Ended up singing loudly when everybody else had stopped. Perhaps I should have done all those trust games after all. Not sure I'll be going back to the group. Maybe. Good people though.

THURSDAY, APRIL 15th

Team meeting at work this morning, led by Maeve who, impossibly, looked even more crumpled and unkempt than usual. Have started to wonder if she's wrestling with something terrible in her life, and has lost hope – that would account for her lack of concern over her appearance. Or maybe it's just that her iron has blown a fuse.

Bumped into James again tonight, running on the Prom. Am worried about this. He's marrying my best friend in a few weeks, and I'm not sure if I took my seafront walk tonight and happened to run into him, or whether I deliberately planned it that way because I know he runs in the early evening. What's going on? Obviously I can't talk to V about this, and would feel awful trying to discuss it with Laura. After all, she's a new Christian, and I'd hate my niggling struggles to disappoint or even devastate her. Must get a grip. Feeling lonely in it all. Not much point in talking to Robert and Nola, they'll be gone soon. Good chat with James. He smiles a lot, which Aaron doesn't, even if he was in a better mood the other day.

FRIDAY, APRIL 16th

After work, went with Laura to the new health club that's opened in Frenton: she had a free guest pass. There must be some kind of promotion going on, because it seemed like half of Frenton was there. Even James and V walked in. She doesn't have an ounce of fat on her perfect body, but apparently they've decided to tone themselves up for the wedding. Couldn't help noticing that James is already looking very toned indeed. I sweated to an Olympic level on the elliptical.

Had a lovely chat with Laura over a post-gym drink. It's strange now that Laura's a Christian. I feel like I should be the one mentoring her, but it's often the other way around. Sometimes I think that I shouldn't tell her about any of my problems. Maybe, if she realises Christians have as many, if not more, issues as other people, it will put her off. I don't want to discourage her, but then I don't want to lie to her either. Christianity can be a hard road; there are moments of elation but there are also times of crushing doubt – at least for me. Admitted that I hadn't prayed for more than a minute or so for months, my prayers these days are more like muttered emergency 999 please help me/please bless me/type prayers. Admitted that I wasn't even sure if I liked God any more. I've been thinking about this a lot recently, and when it comes down to it, sometimes I feel like I've been lied to by the church. There. I've written it down, and no lightning bolts have struck me yet.

Week after week and conference after Christian conference, I've been told that Jesus loves me; that he'll protect me and always be there for me. They say that I am a ray of sunshine in his life and that he went through torture and death just for me. But if he loves me so much, then why did he let my father die in such a brutal way, alone on a dark street? The two things don't seem to fit and I am desperately searching for that third jigsaw piece that allows them both to be true at the same time.

I told Laura all this, and despite being a new Christian, in a way she was the best person to tell. She didn't spout any of those Christian clichés or try to explain some complicated theology, she nodded solemnly and took it all in. Finally she paused and said, ever so gently, 'You believed before all this, didn't you, though you knew that these terrible things happen all the time. That there is poverty and rape and worse things too. And not only that, you believed that all those people should become Christians. That God would help them through their pain. And I don't know if I'm right here, but we follow Jesus, who was brutally executed, the victim of terrible injustice. So surely we don't have any assurance – at least from him – that life will be pain-free or fair?'

Tired now. Will have to think about it.

Arrived spectacularly late at church this morning due to a small mouse problem first thing that had me standing on a chair for a good half an hour. Had the shock of my life when I went to pour my normal breakfast bowl of Special K (for the svelte figure of course) and a little furry ball shot out into my bowl. Panic set in and I spent the next thirty seconds trying to climb my fridge, until I realised it was easier to climb onto the kitchen counter. Then I discovered the mouse was on the kitchen counter so I practically flew across the room to the safety of a chair.

Went to call somebody to help me get rid of it, then realised I didn't have anyone – not a man anyway. There is something very comforting about the presence of a man in a house with a mouse. Aaron would be asleep until noon, so no point in calling him. Thought about calling V but soon remembered that I'd once seen her screaming in tongues at a mouse before shooting out of the room through an open window. Luckily it was on the ground floor, though I get the feeling that she hadn't paid attention. Laura is immensely practical, but I'd feel embarrassed telling her I was rendered useless and a metre up in the air by one little mouse. Would love to call James and have him rescue me. Not a good idea.

Decided I should man up, or rather woman up, and deal with it myself. Later, of course. Ended up running out the room, locking the door behind me and deciding I needed a few hours away from the mouse to come up with a plan.

Then I was even more delayed for church as had to go by and pick up Hayley. Strange, she seemed colder today – maybe the hug I got the other day was my quota for the year. Or the decade. Mrs Tennant was nowhere to be seen – probably still asleep. Hayley wasn't exactly dressed for church, but then the lovely thing about NWCF is that you don't have to dress up. I tried to chat in the car on the way, but all I got was a series of grunts.

It's obvious Hayley has never been taught much in the way of social skills. The usher who greeted us with the usual hug (for me) and handshake (for Hayley) got a shock when she completely ignored his warm good morning and looked at his extended hand with the disdain one usually reserves for something rotting. Then she didn't stand up for the songs, just sat there with her feet up on the hymn book shelf of the chair in front of her, which I think irritated the person in front. During Robert's sermon, she appeared completely bored, and I nearly leaned over to ask her why she'd bothered to come. Glad I didn't, though. At the end, when he prayed, she closed her eyes, and for a moment I thought I saw the hint of a tear in the corner of her eye. Perhaps it was my imagination.

During his sermon Robert said something similar to Nola's comment to me the other day over coffee. He said that a church was about the congregation, not the leader, and it was not a leader that made a church, but rather the church that made the leader. It sounded good, but then I couldn't help but remember all those times when Robert and Nola had kneaded us into shape. It took their strong authority as leaders to deal with the Hemmings, and Robert and Nola were always the ones who checked up on me after Dad's death. I don't think it's because some of the other members of the congregation didn't care, but I think some of them felt nervous, not knowing what to say. In a way, I didn't mind. I didn't know what to say to them either, but Robert and Nola had a knack of saying exactly the right thing. Wish I was like that. So I wondered if Robert and Nola are overstating their case about the role in leadership, in order to ease the pain of their leaving us. I'm not convinced.

A cloud on the horizon – had to miss the post-church cup of tea because Hayley wanted to get home to watch a rerun of *American Idol*, but had a thirty second conversation with Laura that has me worried. Apparently her ex-boyfriend Dave has finished his contract work and is heading back to the UK. He wants to take Laura for 'a meal and a chat.' She doesn't know what to do – and she looks agitated, even though she said that she's fine. *Please God, give Laura wisdom. Don't let anything mess up her life now.*

Drove the still silent and occasionally grunting Hayley home, to be greeted by the lovely Mrs Tennant, who wanted to know if her niece was going to become a duffel-coated nun like me, now that's she'd got all religious, and that if God was there, why did he allow 'itler to breathe, eh? Decided not to engage in a session of apologetics centering around Hitler, and left her house wondering why God allowed Mrs Tennant to breathe. But as I got in the car, Hayley came running out, and called after me. Just two words, that's all.

'Thanks, Helen.' What a strange, sad, confused and confusing girl she is.

Totally forgot I had a mouse problem until I arrived home, so instead settled for locking myself in my bedroom and shoving a towel across the bottom of the door, in case it could slip through the gap. I'm sure that even as I write this I can hear faint rustling noises in the kitchen. Time to buy some new Special K.

Nearly forgot: Robert announced that he and Nola's last Sunday with us will be May 2nd, the weekend before James and V's wedding, so Robert and Nola take off one week, and then V and James will be gone the weekend after, albeit temporarily. Rats. (Yep, I'm obsessed with rodents).

MONDAY, APRIL 19th

Tonight was the first gathering of our leadership appointment committee, and I can tell already that this is going to be about as hilarious as root canal treatment. Boring Brian is on it. Brian the Physics teacher, always droning on about the latest telly appearance of Richard Dawkins (whom he considers may be the Antichrist). I'm not sure whether it's possible to actually be bored to death, but Brian would be excellent if they ever run an experiment. He's single, and likely to stay that way: too much hair; a mad scientist flyaway mop on his head, a beard that could do with some treatment . . . and some nostril hair issues.

And then there's Jonathan Sanger-Brown, a slim older daddy married to Suzi S-B, a blonde yummy mummy who drives a black Mini. Apparently the S-Bs met in a posh church in London, and grew in their love for each other while part of a small fellowship group that served glorious cocktails. Mr S-B often talks about hearing from the Lord, but apparently God hasn't told him that men of his age shouldn't wear cravats. Then there's lovely old Dixie, a delightful Eastender eighty-something who has apparently been placed on the committee to represent the older folk. And V and James make up the complete pack.

In a way I wish that James wasn't in the mix, because then I wouldn't be in close proximity to him. And in another way, I'm glad that James is part of the mix, because I'll be in close proximity . . . This is madness. I've got to get a grip. There's no way I'd actually do anything about these weird thoughts – even if I decided that I was developing a thing for James, I'd die rather than hurt V, or him for that matter. But these fantasy moments are messing up my head. Must kill them.

Anyway, Robert sat us all down, and with an uncharacteristic seriousness, told us that we had all been charged with a solemn responsibility, which made me feel like a jury member on a murder case. He asked Dixie if she would lead us in prayer that we might have wisdom in our deliberations. We all bowed our heads, and waited for the longest time, until finally she said, 'God 'elp us.'

We waited for a bit more from Dixie, further prayerful reflections, some words telling God how vital this all was, in case he didn't know, some quotation from Scripture about the qualifications of a leader . . . V even nodded and mumbled 'Mmm . . .' a couple of times, code for 'That was good, Dixie, give us some more.' But then Dixie said it again, louder this time.

'God 'elp us.'

Robert took the opportunity to end the agony, said *Amen*, thanked Dixie and then, the formal bit over, launched into one of the most amazing speeches I have ever heard. He told us how much NWCF had meant to him and Nola, and how difficult they had found it to make the decision to leave. He said how this had been so much more than a mere job to him – that he had loved and felt genuinely loved by the congregation; that we were an essential part of his life, and he wasn't sure how he would adjust. Then he said that the committee had to make our recommendations without his involvement. This would be tough, he said, because the new leader would be taking responsibility for people that he so dearly cared about – but nevertheless, this was the right way to do things. When he finished, I don't think there was a dry eye. Brian launched into a mini lecture about process, but Dixie cut him off.

'You and Nola are treasures, Robert, and we're gonna be paupers without yer. God help us.'

There was a long pause, and then Robert's shoulders started to shake. He hunched over in his chair, sobbing. James got up and rushed to Robert's side, and knelt beside him, his hand on his shoulder. For a moment, I realised why James and V work. He's so different to her – she's the wacky warrior Queen, and he's the solid rock at her side, always proud of her, even when she's on Jupiter. I remembered again that there was a time when I was worried that I might have to end up marrying James; I didn't want to back then – I thought that God would probably want me with the strong, dependable type, regardless of whether I fancied him or not. I thought I could do a lot better. But as I saw him kneeling with Robert in his pain, I knew that I could have done a lot worse. And I so wanted to not fancy him at all now.

Then V stepped out and stood at Robert's other shoulder. I could tell by the look in her eyes that she had a prophecy coming on. I winced. The last thing Robert needed now was a 'word' that wasn't intelligible to anyone, God included. And then it happened. Dixie was staring straight at V – not in a reproachful way, but with a look that said, 'Not now, darlin'. Not now.'

V seemed to switch gear and prayed the most beautiful, simple, and (thank God) utterly intelligible prayer for

Nola and Robert's future safety, blessing and strength. She thanked God for the imprint that they'd made on her life. It was lovely. Some more prayers were said for Robert, and by the end of them he'd managed to wipe away his tears.

And that was that. Oh, Mr S-B said that a good chum of his from town (town being London, I think) was a management consultant and was sometimes drafted in to help in interviewing situations for key positions. Would we like him to lend us a hand, free of charge, what with us being a Christian organisation? Mr S-B said that his pal was not a Christian, but a 'thoroughly good egg nevertheless.' There was some discussion, which was dull, and I wondered why Christians always expect things to be cheap or free. In the end, his offer was politely declined, as this high level chap would be coming into an environment that was totally alien to him.

Not sure I agreed with that, but couldn't be bothered to object. Brian was nominated as chair of the committee, him being good with process. Once appointed, Brian gave us a lecture about how he was going to set up a committee email 'loop' so that we could communicate more easily as the process moves forward. All minutes, proposals, dates and times of meetings will be shared via the loop. All of this minutiae was explained in way too much detail. At last we adjourned.

I'd just got back to the flat when the phone rang. It was Brian, breathlessly resplendent in his new chairmanship role.

'Listen, Helen' he whispered, as if the phone was bugged, 'I need a bit of advice. When our meeting ended tonight, Robert gave me a letter that had been sent in to the church office. It was marked *Strictly Private and Confidential. For the Attention of the the Leadership Selection Committee*. He hadn't opened it. I've opened it and I'd like to scan it and email it to you. I've got this new Canon scanner which does 16 pages a minute at 730dpi and uses half the ink . . .'

I interrupted Brian, thanked him for the scanner seminar, and asked him who the letter was from. His reply sent a chill down my spine. It was anonymous. As far as I'm concerned, that means that it could only have come from one person: Mrs Hemming.

The scanned copy of the letter landed in my inbox. I read it through quickly, Brian waiting patiently on the phone.

To the chairperson (we trust and pray it will be a chair<u>man</u>, this being in accordance with the divine order of things (Ephesians 5:23))

I write today as one deeply concerned for the welfare of the body of Christ, or as Paul puts it in the King James version in his missive to the Philippians, 'how greatly I long after you all in the bowels of Jesus Christ' (Philippians 1:8).

In recent months I have felt a grieving in my spirit (2 Corinthians 2:5) whenever I have thought about those gathered under the banner of New Wave Christian Fellowship. I have begun to pray that God will once again move in the

*church, and vindicate the faithful elect there that have held fast
to his name and truly seek his glory (1 Peter 1:1)*

*As I have prayed, I have sensed a burden to pray for the removal
of the present leaders of the church, for they, like Diotrephes of old
in his mistreatment of the elder apostle John, (3 John 9) have been
responsible for the severe spiritual famine that has overtaken the
fellowship, prompting some of its most loyal and godly members
to leave the church and seek oasis in spiritual pastures new.*

*Having heard that those aforementioned leaders are now being
relocated, I wanted to write to you today to let you know that
you are indeed in the centre of the purposes of God, and that
you can be assured of my prayers as you seek a godly succes-
sor, even though this letter is unsigned.*

Yours, in bonds,

A watchwoman.

'What do you think Helen? What should I do? The person who wrote this has obviously heard about Robert
and Nola's leaving on the Frenton grapevine. But I don't
want them to see it. Why spoil their final days here?
Should I share it with the rest of the committee?'

I thought about my response for a very long time – half
a second.

'File it where it belongs, Brian. In a fire. As in lake of.
Revelation 20:14.'

After I put the phone down, I wondered what it is that drives an embittered soul like Mrs Hemming. That woman had invested so much emotional energy over the years in being nasty. Part of me scolded myself for jumping to the conclusion that the 'anonymous' letter was from her – we Christians like to believe the best sometimes even when the evidence to the contrary is plain – but the style, the tone, even the reference to the 'loyal and godly' members leaving the church – it had to be her, because she and her long-suffering husband were the only people to have left in a huff in recent years. Robert and Nola were universally loved. When the Hemmings left, we thought that some might get offended with them, and wander off too – but it never happened.

Then I wondered about myself. How different am I from Mrs Hemming, with all my silent chuntering about the flag wavers and my current utter hatred for the youth club kids? Am I a Hemming in training, destined to end my years as a bitter, tetchy whiner?

All this was churning over in my mind, but now I feel sleepy, so need to stop writing. Thanks V. Thanks God. Thanks Brian. That droning voice on the phone probably helped. If I could get Brian to record himself reading Nietzsche I might never have a sleep problem again.

TUESDAY, APRIL 20th

Spent most of the day at work in meetings about departmental reorganisation, which basically means that we are all going to be doing the same things – only with a bigger workload.

Great evening with Laura – we rented *Happy Feet* which cheered me up. Wonderful music and a lot of grinning penguins. Couldn't help thinking about Mr and Mrs Hemming when it came to the part where the traditional elder penguins try to outlaw fun.

Laura has decided to agree to going out for a meal with Dave. We talked about it for a while; she said that their relationship had been difficult, and that she's got no intention of getting back together, but she felt that she owed him a meal and a conversation. Perhaps they could still be friends. I'm not so sure. Perhaps I'm reading between the lines, but I can remember the days when she would come to work with red eyes from too much crying. I got the impression that they had a rocky relationship. It worries me that Laura is so secretive about this area of her life. When I suggested that connecting with Dave might not be the best idea, she got defensive and even said that she might be able to say something to him about God, which might make him a more peaceful and happy person. Then she abruptly changed the subject. Am even more worried now. Their meal is next Saturday – Dave gets in from France that morning, so he isn't wasting any time . . .

After Laura left, Mum called, a little breathless – apparently there have been new developments at the club. The leaders, Mum included, have been working with the police on a weapons amnesty, making the club a place where young people can drop off knives or other weapons and know that they won't get into trouble. I asked her why she hadn't told me about it, and she replied that she didn't want to upset me.

This made me thoughtful. It *would* have upset me, but then again I didn't want my being upset to get in the way of my relationship with other people, especially Mum. Although we still talk a lot and are closer than ever, I feel like there are times when we are both holding back from talking too deeply about Dad.

Anyway – they put a special container where weapons could be dropped off at the youth club, and they got a stash of them. The police were very pleased, and even said it's been one of their most successful weapons amnesties yet. Also, a boy called Martin came to see my mother; crying. He said he wanted to change his life around, that he was sick of the way he was. My mother ended up praying with him and he became a Christian. I suppose my instant reaction is to wonder if it will 'stick', but still, I'm happy for him and for Mum. He's the first person she has ever led to Christ, and she is feeling pleased with herself. Apparently it's all down to this Celtic meditation. Perhaps I should get into something Celtic. Maybe eating porridge for breakfast while listening to Enya would be a start. Must buy a stuffed penguin toy too. Got an email too from the S-Bs asking if I can help out with some baby-sitting.

Met V and Laura for lunch today and told them about the youth club amnesty. V is convinced that it's due to her recent solitary prayer walk. They asked me about Aaron again. Have realised our on/off relationship seems to be off at the moment, so perhaps there's nothing to end: it's all fading away, which is fine. I've called him a few times but he's always busy working on his 'secret' project. Whatever.

Currently sitting on the S-Bs' super comfy corner sofa, which probably has a cashmere cover. Have spent an hour sipping an organic smoothie and reading a trashy magazine. Am happy to help the S-Bs tonight. Apparently their *au pair* ran off with their gardener and, in the words of Suzi S-B, they are in a 'pickle' and I'd be an 'absolute darling' if I could help out. They'd pay double the usual rates of course, which I spent two minutes declining while desperately hoping that they would insist. Thankfully they did. More money than I get paid by the hour as a social worker. I accepted on the spot, despite the fact that Andy, one of their children, may possibly be the incarnation of the devil. Scrap that. Satan is probably terrified of this kid. Am expecting his head to revolve 360 degrees and ectoplasm to flood from his mouth at any moment. Perhaps should wear garlic necklace when baby-sitting for personal protection.

There are three S-B children. Tiffany (11) is constantly sulky mouthed and obsessed by ponies and karate. Her idea of a perfect day out would be to drop kick a few people at a gymkhana. Oscar (8) is by far my favourite, as all he seems to do is stare dreamily out of various windows whilst clutching his teddy bear, Mister Higgins. He's too old for it, but Suzi told me that if I thought Andy was a nightmare, then I should try taking away Oscar's bear.

Andy (6) is currently going through a stage where he is obsessed with sticking his fingers in various things. You name it, he'll insert a digit into it: his mouth, pots of yogurt, dirt, paint . . . and then he wipes his soggy fingers on any unguarded surface, including me. So far this evening I have a trail of sparkly glue, Bolognese sauce and something unidentifiable trailing down the back of my shirt. He makes me want to seal my own womb in case I give birth to a child like him. I finally got him into bed by promising that he could put the dead frog he found in the garden in a resealable plastic freezer bag and sleep with it. It's disgusting but enables me to enjoy extended parking on this plush sofa. It is very comfortable.

Tiffany is still awake and occasionally I hear a few small thumps and thuds, as she is in the gym (the S-Bs have their own in-home exercise room) practising her karate. I didn't have the nerve to send her to bed. I've been watching some of her moves and she certainly seems to pack a punch. I like the S-Bs immensely, they always seem pleasant and kind, but sometimes I wonder if all their wealth and success cushions them from the real world. I saw Suzi S-B nearly break down once because her husband had brought home the wrong sort of Brie from Waitrose. I don't think it's wrong to have money and I happen to know that the Sanger-Browns are very generous to NWCF. But I feel they think that everybody should live as they do, and that they might look down their noses even at my flat – which I love. They can't see how some people could be perfectly happy without the big house and mod cons they have. Ironically, Andy seems perfectly happy with a dead frog and a stick from the garden. Now back to relaxing. I wonder if next time they'd let me have a go in their jacuzzi spa? Mmm. Despite all I've said, soaking in bubbles in the moonlight could contribute to my happiness.

Later

Jonathan and Suzi S-B came back from their little excursion to the latest new restaurant to open in the town. Frenton is hardly Paris, but Suzi said they have great hopes for it. Resolved that after spending time in Mr and Mrs S-B's gorgeous house, I would attempt to make mine more glamorous.

FRIDAY, APRIL 23rd

Went shopping after work and decided to grab a coffee at Marinabean first. Delighted to see James parked on one of the sofas in the corner, and when he saw me, he jumped up, asked me to join him, and bought me a coffee. Apparently he was waiting for V, but then she texted and said she would see him later as, to quote the text,

C u latr am abt my fathrs busness

which probably means that she's got talking to someone about the Lord and couldn't get away. James and I had a lovely long chat and I realised that it was wonderful to talk to a man who didn't try to relate everything to the meaning of life, who was not terribly into German philosophers. James is ordinary, not boring at all. Never did get around to shopping. I returned the favour by buying him a coffee, and finally, after about an hour, V bustled in and began to tell us both about a wonderful 'opportunity to minister' that she'd had. While persuading a parking warden not to give her a ticket, she told him about how Jesus freely forgives our sins. She didn't get the ticket, and he got the gospel. Anyway, the three of us ended up going out for pizza (well, salad as usual for V).

SATURDAY, APRIL 24th

Managed to get round to going for coffee with Aaron which was actually pleasant. He does seem to be on an upper these days. Said again that he was working on an exciting project, but still wanted to keep it hush-hush for the moment. Decided not to try to get into the big chat about us; while he's happier, why spoil things? And right now we're more friends than the vague boyfriend/girlfriend that we used to be, so perhaps my little chat with V and Laura the other day was right – the relationship is heading in the right direction without any big conversation anyway.

Speaking of relationships and conversations, Laura and Dave are getting together tonight for what I think is their scary dinner date. *Lord, please be with Laura. Protect her heart and mind. Have your will in her life. Amen.*

SUNDAY, APRIL 25th

Went to church this morning but couldn't concentrate. Hayley didn't call for a lift and I decided not to phone her, because that might be viewed as pressurising her to come to church, which is certainly not kosher for a social worker, and might incur me the wrath of Maeve.

No Laura at church, which is unusual. Must call her this afternoon. Am worried. Her absence coinciding with Dave's reappearance is not good news.

Next Sunday is Robert and Nola's last, and I know everything is going to be different after they've gone. Phoned Robert last week and asked if he knew what to do if you had a mouse in the house, which was a pathetic attempt to hint that I wanted him to come around and deal with it. Came round the next day with humane traps and this strange gizmo that you plug into a power socket. Apparently it emits a high frequency noise that scares mice away.

Should I buy a cat? Perhaps I'll turn into crazy spinster cat lady Helen Sloane, smelling of urine all the time. Don't like the idea of having a cat flap in the door. Think it would probably allow mice to get in, which I suppose would give the cat something to do . . .

Watching Robert preaching this morning, I meandered into thinking about what it will be like to look up at the platform and not see him there – which in a few days is going to be the case. Decided to hold my hand up in front of me and blot him out; then by squinting my eye, I could see the platform, minus Robert. Unfortunately a enthusiastic lady behind me thought that I was in such raptures because of the preaching that she decided to start muttering, 'Amen, amen.' Robert spotted me and thought that I was trying to ask a question.

'What is it, Helen?' he asked, looking flustered, as we don't usually interrupt sermons with questions, although I can't think why not.

I was embarrassed, and blurted out something stupid about how I was experimenting with blotting him out of the picture because I was going to miss him and Nola so much, so I was trying to prepare myself by hiding him behind my hand and squinting. I said all of this as if it made sense. Robert smiled and then carried on preaching as if there was not a completely insane and possibly dangerous social worker sitting in the congregation.

The worship today was good, but unfortunately we got into that 'This song is working well so let's sing it another 56 times' mode. What was exciting turned turgid. Kristian seemed completely oblivious to the fact that most of the congregation were losing the will to live. At last he allowed us to sing the refrain one last time, and then yelled 'Amen?' into the microphone, to which we all dutifully responded with a united 'Amen!' But I think it was code for 'That's enough, and please don't sing that song again for another 35 years;

can we sit down now please and will you please take an extended vow of silence?' Knowing Kristian, that's one vow that would be broken quickly.

We all sat down, but Kristian wasn't finished. He continued to strum his guitar and give us a lengthy and wholly unnecessary exhortation to be followers of Christ, and not men, which was an obvious reference to Robert and Nola's leaving, although he never made any direct reference to them. The more he spoke, the more he got excited and then he moved into his 'prophetic' voice, which is a spooky version of his real voice. Wondered why some people 'prophesy' things that are patently obvious, and we don't need a word from God about them. Then I wondered if God is as chatty as we make him out to be. Why not tell us the solution to global warming, a cure for cancer or what he thinks about Iraq or the Gaza strip (actually I think I might know what he thinks about the Gaza strip). And then I wondered (Kristian went on for a long time, which gave me plenty of scope for extensive wondering) if what he was saying was correct anyway. I seem to remember Paul the apostle having a very tearful goodbye with his friends at Ephesus when they parted. Yes, ultimately we do follow Jesus, but we do so together with other human beings that we dearly love. Then I wondered why I do so much wondering. Sometimes I look around the church and everyone seems blissfully unconcerned while I'm battling with thoughts that flit around my head like mosquitoes. Wish I could put them on hold. But then I don't want to kiss my brains goodbye. Enough. Tired of wondering about wondering.

Sunday, late

After church, had lunch at Mum's, which was wonderful as usual. The fatted calf lost its life again – what a feast. Ate way too many roast potatoes, which is not good as have bridesmaid's dress fitting this week. Sitting by the fire after lunch made me sad. I looked over at Dad's old chair. Mum never sits there: it's always empty, and I can remember nattering away about all my stuff to him on dozens of previous Sunday afternoons, and then enjoying a nap with the warmth of the fire on my back as I curled up on the rug in front of the fire. And I'd wake up, and he'd be there, sitting, thinking. Took my usual nap, and when I woke up, he wasn't there, and I half expected him to be.

Phoned Laura a few times, but her phone goes right to the answering message. Texted a couple of times too.

MONDAY, APRIL 26th

Laura wasn't at work – apparently she called in sick. No reply to my messages and texts. Plan to stop by her place tonight after work.

At lunchtime went shopping (second attempt) for 'knick-knacks'(where did that phrase come from?) to spruce up my flat a little. Started off in Frenton's only posh department store, then left in a hurry when I found out the average price for a candlestick (minus a candle) was fifty pounds! Ended up in a little store, which was reasonably priced and had some lovely things. Bought some candlesticks, plush cushions, a couple of pictures of Paris to hang on the walls and then splashed out on a cashmere blanket. If the S-Bs can have a cashmere sofa, at least I can have a blanket.

Later

I'm worried. Stopped by at Laura's on the way home from work – and Dave answered the door. Dave is short, but he's solid muscle. His crew cut makes him look like a bouncer, but he does have kind eyes. I started to introduce myself, and he was warm enough, but he didn't invite me in. Just said that Laura had a bad cold, that she didn't want to spread her germs and she'll be back at work in a day or two, he hopes. Then he thanked me for stopping by, and said he'd have her call me when she felt better. And that was it. Not sure if it was my imagination or hyper-sensitivity, or if he closed the door too quickly. Don't know what to do next. Perhaps I should take his word at face value and let her rest and recover.

Later

I tried calling Laura, but got the answering message again. Not good. Hope she's okay. Has Dave moved back in with her?

TUESDAY, APRIL 27th

No Laura still. I think it might be overkill for me to call round there again, if Dave is still there. Sent another text, but no response.

Had a couple of challenging case visits today, including a visit to some foster carers where the relationship has completely broken down. Apparently Justin, the fourteen year old boy they have been looking after, has been driving them insane, completely refusing to be a part of their family. He won't eat with them, barely talks and his room is majorly filthy; he could rent it out for bacterial warfare research. Add non-existent personal hygiene: he stinks. The foster carers are at their wits' end, and can't take any more. Had to get him out of there and into a children's home temporarily. He wasn't pleased, and told me so, accompanying his comments with every swear word that I've ever heard, plus a few that were new. Driving him to the home was a nightmare, as I tried to close my ears to his yelling and my nose to his smell. Placing him into another fostering situation is going to be hard, if not impossible, if he carries on like this.

WEDNESDAY, APRIL 28th

No Laura at work again this morning.

She's dead, I know it. Strangled by her ex-boyfriend in a fit of insane rage and then buried under the patio. Smothered by a pillow, helplessly pinned down by his powerful arms. Shot by a pistol Dave found in Europe while on his travels. Poisoned as she innocently sipped her coffee, unaware of the cyanide Dave had stirred in. Can't believe a second murder has happened in sleepy Frenton.

Lunchtime

Actually, Laura's not dead, just late. She came in at 11am after a doctor's appointment. She said that she'd had a terrible cold but that Dave had been looking after her well over the last few days. They'd had a lovely meal out on Saturday, but she'd explained firmly that she didn't see a future in their relationship, and just wanted to be friends. Apparently he was disappointed but took it reasonably well; asked if he could sleep on the couch for a few days until he decided what to do next. He's got new work in Ipswich starting next week, but he just wanted to crash at her place until then, and he could look after her while she recovered from the cold or flu or whatever it was.

It all sounded fine, and she seems okay, but I've got a niggling doubt about it. She wouldn't lie to me, would she? I did try to find out.

'Are you sure everything's okay?'

'I'm fine, honest. I appreciate your concern, and I'm sorry I didn't get back to you when you texted and called. I hadn't topped up my phone, so I turned it off and didn't get the messages.'

Then she said that the trouble with my profession is that I deal with extreme cases all the time – and then, with what I've been through with my dad, I tend to have a vivid imagination about terrible things happening when in fact everything is fine.

'Don't worry about me. Everything is good. Dave will be off next week. He's got a three month contract, so I doubt if I'll see him for a while.'

All of which should put my mind at ease, but I remember that their relationship had been 'difficult' before. What does 'difficult' mean, and how come she was happy to have Dave dossing down at her place now? Wasn't that risky?

THURSDAY, APRIL 29th

Mad day at work. Laura seems fine, but I'm still concerned.

Had one last final lunch with Nola before they leave. She looked tired. She'd been running around constantly this past couple of weeks, packing, saying goodbye to people and sorting out all the details.

'Are you sure that you're making the right decision, Nola?', I asked. 'This is not just about you and Robert, you know, a lot of people are affected by your move.'

I know. This was over the top, and manipulative, but I'm desperate. Nola was unfazed.

She gave me a kind look and said, in that soft voice I'm going to miss so much, 'I think so. I'm afraid that in life, uncertainty is the only type of certainty we have. I'm going to miss you so much. But it's time we moved on. God's got a new plan for us.'

I nodded but couldn't help feeling miffed that apparently I am not part of that plan. Ordered a double chocolate muffin with white chocolate frosting, in an attempt to eat my way out of pain, which didn't work, but was scrummy. I seem to be getting some of my old appetite back, which may signal the demise of my new svelte (okay, sveltish) figure. Nola said I should enjoy the muffin, she was worried I'd been looking gaunt lately. Can't win, can we? We either look fat or emaciated, or at least I do.

Nola put her hand on my arm.

'I hate goodbyes. I wish I could just sneak out in the middle of the night, like a ghost.'

Wondered about the analogy, as I don't think that ghosts sneak out of places, they tend to hang around and haunt.

'Goodbyes seem so final. But we will be coming back often to visit. I suppose you have to say goodbye before you can meet again.'

At this we both laughed. She sounded like a greeting card with pink kittens on the front. She said that she was thankful to God to have something that made saying goodbye so hard.

I suddenly realised one of the many reasons I like Robert and Nola so much. Even though they are my leaders I feel like we are genuine friends. She wasn't coming for lunch so that she could comfort me, she came so I could comfort her. They always made me feel valuable, that my opinion and input were respected.

Still no sign of the mouse. Maybe I won't have to be Helen 'crazy cat lady' Sloane after all. Relieved. Thought about telling Nola about my feeling a twinge of something for James (I know that 'a twinge of something' is vague, but that's what it is), but decided not to. I can pull myself together. If I can get through the last eighteen months, I can certainly control myself and let V and James get on with having a wonderful life together. I'll shut whatever the 'something' is down. That's that. Sorted. I hope.

After work I met V and we went to Frenton's one and only bridal shop for my dress fitting. I am the lone bridesmaid. The dress is as gorgeous as I had hoped from looking at the photograph, and I think it suits me. The roast potatoes from Sunday and the white chocolate muffin indulgence probably helped contribute to the need for a couple of seams to be very slightly adjusted, but I absolutely love the look.

This evening went for walk along the Prom with Aaron, who was back to his usual sullen self. Tried to kick start a conversation by asking if he had any news, and he said that the news was that all news is of no consequence when one looks at the big picture of cosmic history. A hundred thousand years from now nothing will be remembered from what is now anyway. Regretted asking. Obviously Aaron's new project isn't going too well, whatever it is. He'll be onto something more interesting soon. Wish he'd grow up and get a life. We are definitely just friends now. Maybe even that's fading too. Felt frustrated that my lovely time with V at the dress fitting was overshadowed by Aaron being himself.

SATURDAY, MAY 1st

Ditto walk as per yesterday, minus Aaron, which was an improvement, sad to say.

SUNDAY, MAY 2nd

I've been dreading this evening for ages now – ever since Robert and Nola announced that they were leaving, the prospect of saying goodbye has been hanging over me like a rain cloud. They've been so wonderful. I've heard so many stories about Christian leaders who are uncaring, dictatorial, manipulative and egotistical, but Robert and Nola have been none of those things. Robert has been a clear, firm leader – which is exactly what we've needed – but he has led with kindness and encouragement; I always feel that what he says is so well thought through. They are both . . . so sensible. And Nola is an absolute angel. I'm going to miss our cups of coffee in Marinabean. I hope that we'll be able to stay in touch.

They are going to team up with another couple – apparently they were at Bible college together years back. A church plant was started on a housing estate in Warrington about two years ago, and things have grown so well that they need some more help. Robert's mix of teaching and pastoral gifts makes him a perfect fit, and he's often said that if they moved church, he would want it to be more than a job move – he wants to do ministry with people that he feels 'joined in heart' with, to use his phrase, and these pals from college days seem to fit that bill.

Anyway, the farewell service was a tearjerker. Brian led the service through, which went smoothly enough. There was an 'open mike' time when people were invited to come up and say some parting words of thanks or tribute to Robert and Nola, whatever they wanted. Mr S-B said some very appreciative things about Robert being one of the best leaders he's ever known, which was high praise indeed from someone who spends so much time in the corporate world. He said Robert had excelled in leading the most potentially difficult 'workforce sector' that there is – the band of volunteers that make up the local church. 'You can't hire them, fire them, demote them, or cut their wages' said Mr S-B, 'but you can inspire them, and that's exactly what you've done, and we will all be forever grateful.'

Dixie came forward, a broad smile on her face: 'Most of you know that I didn't bump into Jesus until I was 73, which was daft of me. So Robert, you've been the only vicar I've ever known. So I want to say that if I had met Christians like you when I was a kid, I might not 'ave 'ad such a misspent and wayward youth in the East End. Mind you, I wouldn't have missed some of that misspent wayward stuff for the world . . .' – and then she winked, and sat down.

There was an odd moment when V went to the microphone, which perhaps is to be expected. She was tearful and thanked Robert for keeping her balanced and normal (which is a stretch). She also had some lovely things to say about Nola. One of the beautiful things about V, with all her weirdness, is that she notices. She seems not just to see people, but to study them, because she is genuinely interested. She put her finger on some of Nola's strengths with some well chosen words. But then came the odd bit.

V had a small brown bag in her hand, and had some plastic toy sheep in it. After she'd finished saying appreciative things, she paused and said 'I do feel led, not only to pray for Robert and Nola as they leave, but for us as we stay. They have been such fabulous shepherds to this flock. I was reading the Bible this morning and came upon the text that says, "Strike the shepherd, and the sheep will be scattered." Obviously no one's striking Robert, but our shepherd is leaving, and right now there's not another shepherd ready to step into his shoes.'

With this she paused (I'm not sure whether this was for dramatic effect or just hesitation) and scattered the plastic sheep around the front of the church. 'I am not prophesying that we will be scattered – but I want Robert to pray for us, that this will not happen, that we'll stay together, that our unity will be maintained through the tough journey that we have as we look for another leader.' It was almost normal, although it did look like a plastic sheep version of the Texas chainsaw massacre.

Robert took the microphone, and prayed quietly and specifically for us in our future. He seemed to take what V said seriously. I'm still confused about it all, because it did put a dampener on the evening. A shred of fear crept into the atmosphere, and things weren't as light and easy after that. I'm not sure whether V was wise or wacky in doing what she did; but then I live my whole life wondering if V is wise or wacky. Maybe she's a bit of both at the same time.

Then Robert preached his final sermon to us. He spoke on the text, 'little children, love one another.' He told a story about the Apostle John. Apparently, in his final years, the old man would keep repeating the same thing whenever he preached, 'Love one another.' It got to the point where his congregations got tired of it. But John was unshakable. This was his life message. Robert said that, in a way, the sentence that John used sums up everything that matters, because it's not just 'love one another' – that statement doesn't have to be especially Christian – but rather 'little children . . . love' As we remember we are children of God, and experience his power, grace and transformation in us, so a love that is beyond human capacity can be among us. Powerful stuff.

Then we prayed for Robert and Nola, and the service was over. There were the obligatory cups of tea, some wine and some of the most marvellous cakes in the history of the Christian church. The evening ended with a presentation of a gift to Robert and Nola – a cheque from an offering we've been collecting. And then they were gone. When they left, it was like a bride and groom leaving the reception for their honeymoon. Everyone followed them out to the car and waved them off; no one wanted to say goodbye. They won't be leaving town for another couple of days, and I've offered to help with some of the packing up of the house before the removal van arrives, so at least I'll get to see them again before they go.

Laura was there, and seemed fine. I think maybe she might be right – perhaps my job tends to make me neurotic and fearful. Glad she's not under the patio though.

TUESDAY, MAY 4th

I can't believe it. I had planned my early morning walks so carefully so as to assure myself that I was not on the lookout for James. And so what does he do? Change his running schedule, that's what. I was striding along the Prom sweating in my tracksuit, when he jogged up behind me.

We nattered for a while about nothing much, and it was then that I decided to tell him. It was as if he'd been expecting me to say something big. I hadn't anticipating seeing him, so I was unprepared.

'James, there's something I want you to know. Before you and V got together, you were my closest friend. You were thoughtful, loyal, an amazing all round friend, and I love you for that. I got to know you very well indeed.

– 78 –

And that's why . . .' I hesitated, and obviously stifled a tear. 'And that's why . . .'

James looked thunderstruck, obviously wondering what on earth was coming next.

'And that's why I want you to know, even though we won't ever be that close again, I'm so thankful for you being a friend who helped me, at least to begin to get through the hell of losing Dad. I'll always be grateful. V has found herself an amazing man, and I'm so happy for you both. I know you're going to be great together.'

And that was that. I'm glad he didn't hug me, seeing as I was sweaty. I felt like I'd drawn a line, and put things in order without creating a big mess as I did so. He seemed very pleased.

Lunchtime

Call me neurotic, but I am certain that Laura isn't telling me the whole story. She said that we can get together later in the week, but there's something up. The banter and chat that we usually enjoy at work is all but shut down, and I've noticed that, when she's not answering the phone or directing visitors, she seems to be staring into space.

Feel good about James. I think that in choosing to do what's right, rather than being drawn to do what's wrong, that I'm in a good place with myself – and with God.

Spent this evening on a marathon final clean-up over at Robert and Nola's place. The house they're moving to in Warrington is smaller than the one here, so our local charity shop has been getting a lot of good stuff. They're leaving very early tomorrow morning so as to miss the worst of the M25. Nola gave me a beautiful print of one of Salvador Dali's 'La Biblica' series; the line drawing of Peter, standing on a rock, the keys of the kingdom in his hand.

'I love this piece. It's so not the Dali that everyone thinks of, with his squishy clocks and giant eggs and all that. Peter looks so ordinary, so vulnerable, and yet he is strengthened by the knowledge that Jesus not only loves him but also trusts him, even though he knows he will fail. Apparently a friend of Dali's commissioned him to create the series, in the hope that studying biblical characters would prevent him from going insane. Our mad world needs to know that love. Warrington needs to know, which is why Robert and I are tearing ourselves away from here, and from dear friends like you. Hold steady. You have a solid rock under you that you can't see. You've come so far. Don't sink, girl. I love you.'

I hugged them for way too long in what was something like a rugby scrum, and we all cried, and then, at last, I left them to spend their last night in Frenton . . . now the house is cleared they are going to stay at a bed and breakfast.

WEDNESDAY, MAY 5th

Am possibly losing my mind as when I left work I drove over to Robert and Nola's for a cup of tea, forgetting that they're not there any more. Am still worried about Laura and have no one (well, no leader) to talk with about it.

Came home and made tea, spent a long time staring at Dali's drawing of Peter. I wonder if Peter ever wandered back to any of the Galilean haunts where he had spent so much time with Jesus, perhaps hoping for yet another post-resurrection appearance from his friend? Maybe even years after Jesus ascended?

THURSDAY, MAY 6th

Drove over to Robert and Nola's again, this time in the full knowledge that they weren't there. Sat outside their dark, empty house, a place that had been so warm and filled with laughter and now is so cold, bleak even. Shed a few more tears, and drove home. Need to get a grip.

FRIDAY, MAY 7th

Wedding tomorrow. No time to write this – got to get to the wedding practice.

SATURDAY, MAY 8th

Hoping to get to have a good chat with Laura at the wedding reception this evening. James and V have invited Aaron, which is kind of them. They don't know him very well, but V said that she was praying that he'd be impacted for the gospel by their nuptials. Not sure I can believe that will happen.

Peter looks lovely hanging over my fireplace, if you know what I mean. I like Peter a lot, because he walked on the water and then got wet. Sounds a lot like me.

SUNDAY, MAY 9th

Yesterday's wedding was great – at least it started that way. Compared to the hen-party it was a restrained affair and I enjoyed it. I was prepared for V's usual surreal free for all, where Bible verses fight Enya songs for supremacy, and the first dance is an interpretive jazz presentation of the crucifixion. But there was no Enya or crucifixion. I found the ceremony beautiful, and I loved my dress. As I was walked down the aisle Laura took one look at me in my dress and tears welled up in her eyes. I'd like to think that this eruption of emotion was because I looked so stunning, but I couldn't help thinking there and then that she's right on the edge with her nerves and emotions . . .

V, of course, looked beautiful. She was beaming, from ear to ear, and James looked gorgeous.

Seeing as Robert and Nola are gone, and felt that it would crazy to make a return trip a few days after they'd left, Brian led the ceremony, which was fine as the actual legalities were sorted by having a registrar in attendance. Am glad to report that Brian's nostril hairs had been evacuated for the nuptials, which was a relief, because they were getting to the point where I was going to offer to braid them with beads. His welcoming comments at the beginning were too long, so my mind wandered into a daydream about how ridiculous it would have been for me to marry Aaron. More of a dreamette . . . He'd probably turn up drunk and then yell at the vicar. In fact as a new born atheist he would probably refuse to get married in a church at all. I'm not sure he even believes in marriage.

He's changed so much. I remember at University, when he was in his passionate Christian phase, he sat me down and told me that everybody should get married as soon as possible to avoid sin. He said that this was his plan, because he was worried that his weak flesh wasn't strong enough to withstand 'the burn.' Aaron tends to take himself way too seriously no matter what it is he's doing. Leading the CU or espousing the merits of Nietzsche on a packed number 3 bus, he believes a hundred and ten percent in it. Hoped he would behave himself at the reception.

James delivered a speech that was heartfelt and sweet. He genuinely seems stunned to find himself in love with and loved by V. I was so glad we'd had our chat on the Prom. During the ceremony V had asked Brian to bind her and James's hands together as a sign of their eternal love – the one exception to an otherwise fairly normal wedding. Unfortunately he tied the knots far too tight, and they had to be cut free with scissors so they could sign the register.

The reception was held at The Pavilion, Frenton's swanky seafront hotel, and turned out to be a ceilidh; much fun was had by all as we took it in turns to spin each other across the room. I only had a couple of glasses of sloe gin, which must be mainly fruit, surely, but maybe the emotions of the day exhausted me, and I didn't eat much. Anyway, for some reason, by the end of the evening I was mostly draped over Aaron, who took it in turns to either stroke my neck or drink from his glass of wine. It was silly, because we are just friends now, but these things happen at weddings, and I had never got round to formally saying that the boyfriend/girlfriend thing was over. It must have been my absent minded daydreaming during the ceremony that did it, but I asked him pointedly whether he ever thought of getting married one day, and he replied obliquely that even if he was a Siamese twin he would still be alone. Then he grabbed my hand and whirled me off for another time of flinging me at the nearest wall.

A little later I took my chance to have a chat with Laura, and I think that the emotion of the wedding must have disarmed her, because my fears were confirmed. There's no pleasure for me in the discovery that I'm not a neurotic social worker after all, but that my intuitions were right.

It turns out that Laura was covering up because of a potent mixture of fear and shame. The initial meal with Dave had been good, too good. He'd managed to sweet talk his way into her bed, where they'd spent a passionate night together. The next morning she woke up to the realisation that not only had she had sex with a man that she didn't love, but also one who frightened her – turns out that Dave would occasionally slap her when they were together before. Anyway, she didn't waste any time in telling him that their night together had been a terrible mistake, and that she didn't want to continue the relationship. He then resorted to previous form, only worse – he punched her in the lower chest, bruising her ribs. And then he'd announced that he'd camp out at her house as long as he chose to – and if she told anyone, he'd hurt her. Hence the three days off work with a 'cold' and the visit to the doctors – she was concerned that she might have a fractured rib, which an X-ray proved was not the case.

She'd felt too ashamed and foolish to admit to any of this, and just wanted to be rid of him – and all the emotions of the wedding had brought it to the surface. V and James were so obviously in love – such a sharp contrast to the viciousness of Dave.

'He's gone for good now, and I've had the locks changed to make sure he can never come back. He basically kidnapped me in my own home, but I could never prove anything, so there's no point in involving the police. What matters is that he's out of my life for ever. I hate him.' She cried a lot. I'm so relieved that the truth is out, and felt so bad for her. She must have been terrified. I hate Dave too. And I only met him once. Kind eyes? I got that wrong. I hope that V and James didn't notice any of our intense, tearful conversation. I'd hate anything to have spoilt their day.

Finally V and James were waved off to embark on their honeymoon (fruit picking in Mexico, to connect with

God's bounty). Laura left, said she needed to get some sleep. So I had a glass of wine (which may not have mixed with the gin too well) – and that's when I made the big mistake. Aaron asked me if I wanted to go back to his flat for a coffee, and I decided that this would give me the opportunity to finally tell him we were formally finished, and just friends now.

I woke up this morning on a chair in Aaron's flat with a splitting headache. At first I wondered what on earth had happened last night, and then remembered coming to the flat. And after that, all I had done was to slump into one of Aaron's tortuously uncomfortable armchairs and go out like a light. Aaron was sparked out on the sofa. Looking at him, he was thin and vulnerable, lying fully clothed with his knees tucked into his chest and his long hair falling over his cheeks, covering his eyes.

The flat was a mess. And then I noticed a large sheet of paper above his desk, with lots of of post-it notes, each one with a name written on it. I crept over and looked closer and immediately recognised the names of some of the kids who attended the youth club. There were strange diagrams that spiralled off into question marks; bizarre symbols and writing that looked like the tip of the felt pen had been pushed so hard that it had ripped through the paper.

Aaron was playing detective. He was trying to solve my father's murder, and from the looks of his wall of suspicion, he was obsessed with it. I don't know where he was getting his information from – perhaps he'd been chatting with the kids around town, trying to find out if there were any whispers on the streets. From the looks of his wall, he hadn't got very far – just managed to identify that there were four or five kids who hung out together a lot – perhaps he thought that if he could spot a gang, it might lead him to find out if they had been involved.

I knew he was finding it difficult to deal with the events of that night, but I didn't know it had come to this. I was confused. All the feelings about how it was partially his fault that Dad was gone came flooding back. And now he was trying to solve the case. This was the trail of new discovery, the secret project that he had been so excited about before – and had hidden from me. I'm not sure why I felt so angry about it – after all, he was only trying to help. Maybe it was because he had kept me out of the loop.

I feel so helpless about Dad's murder, and now, after the first flurry of inquiries, I barely hear anything from the police. I get the impression that the case has gone cold, and there is no progress – even that they are embarrassed at not being able to solve a murder in a small town like Frenton. The gang, they believe, were from out of town and fled straight after the murder. Anyway, I feel abandoned by the police, and now Aaron has been sneaking around trying to sort something out that affects Dad without talking to his daughter.

Suddenly Aaron stirred on the couch. He blearily opened his eyes and must have clocked what I was looking at immediately. 'Helen' he spluttered, his voice still croaky from sleep. 'I . . . thought that if we could have some closure . . . if we could find out who did it, then it would be over. I wanted you to be happy again . . .'

I began tearing down the pieces of paper on the wall and told him that we were finished. Tears were pouring down my face, smudging my already ruined eye make-up. Then I grabbed my bag and ran out of the room. I had to get away from the yellow post-its and the stale smell of cigarettes.

As I slammed the front door behind me, I collided with the last person I wanted to see – Mrs Hemming and her ugly dog. I must have looked a right state, mascara smeared down my face, my dress creased and scruffy. She shot me a look of horror, mingled with disgust – the one she uses for most things.

I'll think about her later. Now all I want to do is have a bath, put on my pjs and go back to sleep. No church this morning, for about three hundred reasons.

Later

Have recovered from my dramatic exit from Aaron's flat. I am currently wrapped up in a large fluffy towel, supping a cup of peppermint tea, surveying my gleaming flat. I decided to do a frenetic clean-up before I had my bath – there's no point in washing myself and then slouching around in a dirty flat. I have even lit one of the candles V left when she was last here and am feeling vaguely human again.

I don't know what to think about Aaron. I know he was trying to help me, but I hate that he was doing it secretly. I'm glad I've clarified our relationship now. Am not even sure that I have the energy to be his friend.

And then there's my unfortunate encounter with Mrs Hemming. Will she keep quiet about it? Some hope. What an opportunity for gossip, covered in 'I am only sharing this for prayer . . .'! It will probably be only a matter of time before she feels 'moved by God' to spread it around the town. And who's going to believe me that it was perfectly innocent?

I'm trying to work out if I care if she does start. Why should my reputation matter to me – is it because I am worried about how my behaviour might look as a Christian (and a member of the search committee at that)? Or am I afraid that the news will reach the ears of future suitors and they'll decide not to date such a Jezebel? If they do, perhaps I don't want to date them in the first place. Surely if a man truly falls in love with me, he won't care about rumours? Have decided that I'll deal with Mrs Hemming if and when she talks.

An email landed from Brian tonight, reminding us all that we have a selection committee meeting tomorrow night to meet our first applicant. His CV was attached. Must try to read it before the meeting.

Have calmed down a bit more since discovering Aaron's amateur detective work. I suppose, thinking about it, he was trying to do the only thing he could to help. He can't bring Dad back, but he could do something to bring the killers to book.

Laura seemed okay today, but still looks tearful. I think the whole Dave debacle shook her up. I hope she means it when she said that it's over for good – have seen too many cases at work where people in abusive relationships keep coming back for more. Had lunch with her and let her talk some more about her anger with Dave. She feels stupid for letting him get anywhere near her again, and vows that he's history.

Had a heart-rending job to do this afternoon, which put my nagging worry about Mrs Hemming and my concerns about Aaron into perspective. I had to visit some clients who have been long term foster carers for a baby, Rosie, born addicted to heroin because her mother was. Tony and Sandra have had Rosie as their own since she was a week old – we had to take her into care immediately because her mother was in no fit state to care for her. Anyway, we've been looking for a permanent adopter. Tony and Sandra talked about taking that role, but didn't feel it was right to assume that long term responsibility at their age – they'd be in their early sixties when Rosie is 18. Then we located a suitable adoptive family. And so today was the handover. It was traumatic. They have poured out such love and care, and it was like they were now having to give their own child away to a stranger. There were loads of tears and farewell kisses. As far as I know, Tony and Sandra have no faith, and yet they tirelessly give themselves and allow their hearts to be broken. Next time I hear a preacher say that the church is the only beacon of love in a loveless world, I think I'll respond by slapping them. Not very loving . . .

The selection committee's first interview took place tonight. We interviewed a Mr Gordon Bleasdale, a very large man. Not much to say about him. Pleasant enough – maybe a bit bland. I didn't chime in much, as I didn't get round to scanning the CV, and I didn't want to ask a question that would make that obvious. We decided to have a second interview with him Wednesday night. Missed V and James; hope they're enjoying their honeymoon. Must confess to a heady sense of power, being part of the group who will recommend the new minister to the church. Must remember to stay humble. Is it okay to be proud of being humble? Sounds like that would mean that you weren't humble at all. There I go again . . .

Aaron texted me tonight and apologised again, and promised to leave me alone for a while to think. I texted back *Good idea. But we're still friends, aren't we? Sorry if I overreacted. I know you were trying to help. Catch up soon.*

He's just texted back. *Friends always Helen. Thanks.*

Mmm. *Friends always* does sound like a long haul. Glad we've reconnected though.

Worship leader Kristian (i.e. floppy-haired, twaddle-talking, inappropriate-touching, guitar-playing Kristian) is being his usual idiotic self again. He phoned Laura to tell her that God has given him a new destiny, to lead Christians everywhere against the scourge of poverty. It sounds very noble: God has given Kristian a 'word' that he will be a leader of men (apparently women have nothing to contribute) and he will end world poverty by 2020, perhaps with help from Bono and Barack Obama.

Kristian being Kristian, he's written a special song called *The bleeding poor* and wants Laura to help him film a music video of him and some children in the church hall. Apparently it is a powerful song of action, and when people hear it they will take to the streets and end poverty. When Laura asked him exactly what it was he was planning to do for the poor, he muttered something vague about breaking their iron bonds and wanted to talk about his concept for the video instead.

His new project sounds harmless enough – how far wrong can you go trying to help the poor? Actually, I think it's possible to go very wrong indeed. But his idea has even made me feel guilty. I can't even remember the last time I gave to charity, apart from the church, or even thought much about those people less fortunate than myself. In fact, these days, when I spot a magazine or newspaper article about the developing world, I tend to skip over it. I have enough problems of my own without worrying about other people's stuff. Selfish or practical?

Selfish, I think. Anyway, we'll see. Watch out hurting world, Kristian's on his way to save you . . .

Nola called tonight. She and Robert are settling in well, and love it. Apparently there's a girl in the church there called Hazel. Nola says she's like me – and they are going to be great friends. Felt jealous. I'm glad that things are going well for them, sad for us. Somehow it feels wrong that they should be happy without us.

WEDNESDAY, MAY 12th

Bit of a crisis this morning because Justin, the smelly lad who I had to place in a children's home, did a runner last night and is nowhere to be found. Had a conversation with the police but they seem to think that he'll turn up in a day or two: kids of his age go walkabout all the time. Couldn't help thinking that I hope they'd do a better job with Justin being missing than they did with my dad's case.

Went to church for the second interview with Gordon Bleasdale this evening and nearly died of a laughter-induced hernia – *before* the interview started. I now find it impossible to take anything that Kristian says or does seriously. I walked into the church hall, and found a group of children from the church's Sunday school, fully blacked up in some sort of brown camouflage paint, holding spears and wearing rags. You couldn't make this up.

When I asked them who they were supposed to be, they seemed confused. One little boy said he thought he was a Zulu warrior until Kristian himself came bustling in, dressed in black Levi jeans and a scarlet T-shirt with the the face of a crying child printed on it. He looked like a cult leader and corrected the Zulu warrior: 'You represent the world's poor – now get back into your position.'

I looked around for Laura and eventually discovered her behind a pillar, clutching a video camera with a shaking hand. 'I can't believe he's blacked them up. Oh Helen, it's so funny but sick and inappropriate as well – he's even got them lying on the floor, rubbing their bellies and groaning. What on earth does he think he's doing?'

'Time to roll again' commanded Kristian, propping one of his legs up on a church pew, trying to be manly and director-like. 'Children . . . places!'

After he'd barked a few more orders, Kristian got up and positioned himself on the small stage at the front of the church, the children gathering around him. Laura switched on a backing track and Kristian began lip-syncing to the song as around him the children dropped one by one to the floor, clutching their stomachs and moaning. As he carried on singing, he touched each child on the forehead. They then magically recovered and sprang up, smiling and making strange noises that I think were supposed to be some sort of tribal language.

Suddenly the door at the back of the church opened, and a family walked in – a man, wife, and two children, a girl and a boy. And it was obvious that their family history did not begin in Frenton. Sub-Saharan Africa, from the looks of things. They looked wide-eyed at Kristian and the smiling faces of the painted kids. But Kristian, lost in the moment, began to sing some of the worst lyrics ever:

Listen child, lost, downtrodden
Your eyes they flood with tears
Is there anyone who cares
To comfort you in so many fears

God loves you, you, YOU!

Listen child, so lonely now
Lift your eyes to the skies
On wings of eagles you will rise,
And soar, you'll weep no more . . .

God loves you, you, YOU!

Perhaps bolstered by the fact that he now had a larger audience with the arrival of the African family, and utterly oblivious to the fact that they were black, he launched into the terrible chorus:

The bleeding poor, the bleeding poor
They have less and we have more
The bleeding poor, the bleeding poor
They have less and we have more . . .

Suddenly the man interrupted. 'Excuse me, what is this?' he inquired, firmly, but not unkindly. 'Is this a church?

We are new to this area, and we are Christians. Is this New Wave Christian Fellowship?'

'It is', said Kristian, and then, as if his next statement would fill this family with delight, 'We're making a video about making poverty history. I'm the worship leader here, and I've written a song . . . well, the Lord has given me a song . . . about the bleeding poor.'

I tensed, and waited for the reaction of acute offence that would explode from this visitor as he saw the daubed faces of all these white kids, being set free by a warbling white boy. But no anger came. The man threw back his head, and the hall filled with the sound of his rich laughter. And that was the last straw for me and Laura. We collapsed in giggles. It was lovely to see Laura laughing. I haven't heard that full-on laugh of hers since the Dave disaster.

After that stunning performance, the ministerial interview with Gordon Bleasdale was an anti-climax. Brian delayed the meeting by fifteen minutes so that we could have a chat and get to know this new family, I hope they start coming to the church. I love the sound of this man's laugh. His wife was shy, but I get the feeling she would soon warm up. They are David and Grace Kyomo; their children are Esther and Edward. They've moved to Frenton from London; just arrived, and one of their first priorities is to find a church. A friend of a friend of theirs back in 'town' knows Dixie, and suggested they try NWCF.

The interview ended with us inviting Mr Bleasdale to preach for us this coming Sunday.

No rumblings from the Hemmings' direction. Perhaps I'm okay. Perhaps not, more likely.

Thought about sending Aaron an *Are you okay?* text to check in again. Decided against it.

THURSDAY, MAY 13th

Bit worried about the large man (sorry, Mr Bleasdale). He unsettles me for some reason and I'm not sure we should have asked him to come to preach. I have a bad feeling about this. His answers to our questions were okay, but sometimes it felt like he was reciting from a textbook, rather than speaking from the heart. Although I'm a little worried that I am being sizeist, and judging him because he's big.

FRIDAY, MAY 14th

The police called and Justin has turned up. He went off with a bunch of mates and ended up sleeping rough under the pier for a couple of nights. Unfortunately the underside of the pier does not have shower facilities, so he's as smelly as ever. Stopped by the children's home and he was his usual verbose and unpleasant self. Placing him in foster care is going to be a challenge.

SATURDAY, MAY 15th

I have decided that when I relax, I feel guilty. Spent a nice morning over at Mummy Kitty's for coffee and chat, and then decided to head for home and curl up with a book for the rest of the day. Kept fighting a restless and vaguely guilty feeling that I should be doing something 'useful' instead. Mad when you consider that in the Old Testament God specifically commanded his people to rest on the sabbath. For some reason I find it easier to 'rest' doing frantic religious things than to chill out doing nothing. Must learn to relax. I wonder if there are relaxation classes available that don't involve breathing exercises and humming?

SUNDAY, MAY 16th

I feel like Simon Cowell, except that I'm not male, rich, on the television or in the music industry. Nevertheless, as a fully fledged member of the NWCF Leadership Selection Committee (not as catchy as *Pop Idol*, I know, but it still involves judging), I gave a definite and hearty thumbs down to Bleasdale, the first candidate who came to 'try out' for the position of leader of our church. It's odd that the trying out bit involves preaching. I understand it's very important that the person who is going to do most of the preaching is slightly more interesting than watching paint dry, but it does seem strange that this is the main criterion we judge them by. I wouldn't want an amoral or serial killing pastor who nevertheless was good on Leviticus. And this trying out stuff has made me wonder about how we treat preaching. Is it something that Christians have to have, as part of their gatherings? Is it an entertainment or a sport? Sometimes I hear Christians talking about preaching in the same way people talk about bands. Just what is great preaching anyway?

I digress. What we had today, however, was not great preaching, except perhaps in the eyes of the preacher. Mr Bleasdale was the very large man in a very large suit, who had seemed friendly and normal in our two interviews with him. He had intelligent but wooden answers to questions, a great theological education, and has done well in leading his last church, which hasn't either exploded in growth, nor dwindled in decline. Dixie remarked that seeing as so many of the church were ancient like her, and her generation are popping their clogs at high speed, it is amazing these days that the churches aren't emptier than they are. We'd ended the second interview feeling neither arrested nor appalled, and decided that we'd ask him to preach – and were taken aback when he offered to come this Sunday, without consulting his own church. Perhaps that's what was niggling away at me earlier this week: the impression that he was a law unto himself, and that he lacked sincerity.

Anyway, it was fine till he started speaking. He was affable when meeting people before the service started, and shook as many hands as he could. But something happened to him the moment he stood behind the lectern. Suddenly his voice took on an affected tone, really pompous, and it got louder and louder as he went on –

particularly when his points were weakest. He seemed to take great delight in telling us what the original Greek meant, and also did a bit of name dropping, casually mentioning a few minor celebrities in the small goldfish bowl of the Christian world, that he'd rubbed shoulders with. He'd quote a famous commentator by saying, 'as my good friend says' and then name them – I bet he'd barely met them. And his attempts to be impressive were the opposite.

He became slightly more normal again over the post-preaching cups of tea, and then left so we could vote. I wrote a large *Not on your life* on my piece of paper (we committee members only bring recommendations to the congregation and have no more voting power than any-one else). The vote was conclusively negative. Only 32% thought that the Greek-quoting friend of the Great and Famous was for us. Am relieved. But still we need a leader. Robert and Nola have been gone for a couple of weeks now, and there's no replacement in sight. I know it's early days yet, but Robert and Nola played such a vital role in leading us – I'm worried that we won't do well without them. Can't help wishing that Robert could have stuck around to help us through this transition process, but I understand that's not normally the way these things are handled. Feel a niggling anxiety about the church – hope that we are going to do well with this tricky journey, without Robert and Nola's calming influence to hold us steady.

The Kyomo family showed up, which was lovely, hope they weren't put off by our big fat Greek scholar. (I must stop this sizeist talk. I know it's wrong, but I have a problem with gigantic preachers who blether on about self control and then can't lay off the doughnuts). Back to the Kyomos. Grace is one of those ladies who seems to have a permanent smile. She's beautiful, and her smile seems genuine. And Dixie got Mr Kyomo laughing again, I think she was being a bit saucy over the cup of tea. I wandered over to them, welcomed them again and apologised for Kristian's appalling video shoot performance. Mr Kyomo said he hadn't laughed so much in ages, and started laughing again. I like these people. Esther and Edward came bounding out of their Sunday school classes with beautifully crayoned drawings of Moses in hand, and it was obvious that they had enjoyed themselves. Good news.

Brian emailed a few other applications for the leadership selection committee to review. Seems like there are a few people who'd like to come to Frenton.

MONDAY, MAY 17th

Brian called tonight. I am seriously thinking about asking him to record his voice. He could make a fortune and bring happiness to insomniacs everywhere. But I snapped wide awake when he explained the reason for his call. 'I've got two items of bad news – and I'm worried because one of these is bad news for you.' I gulped. I've had enough bad news to last a lifetime; I suddenly felt that surge of panic that rises when you feel that one extra stress could topple you over the edge.

Brian explained that, following the No vote for Bleasdale, some of those who had voted for him were not exactly thrilled. A few emails had arrived, concerned that the church had missed its opportunity to have 'deeper' teaching from a man who 'so obviously has been treading the corridors of evangelical influence for some time.' Some felt that the church could benefit from his experience and connections. But it was the second bit of bad news that floored me. Dutifully fed into the scanner by Brian, the message made my heart beat very fast indeed.

To the chairman of the leadership selection committee, New Wave Church.

It having come to my attention that your committee includes one Helen Sloane among its membership, I have decided with regret that it is my painful Christian duty to inform you that the aforementioned Miss Sloane was discovered in a highly compromising and (it would seem) immoral position recently. The Apostle Paul speaks plainly about expelling the immoral believer – but apparently in New Wave, the guilty are not only not disciplined, but invited to continue to have responsibility.

Miss Sloane was seen leaving the home of a young man in the very early hours of the morning. We are given to understand that this youth is not a follower of Christ, thus creating the possibility of a union with Belial. It so happens (although we do not put our faith in the power of coincidence, Romans 8:28) that a fellow believer was in the area, and thus Miss Sloane's inappropriate behaviour was noticed. I hope that you will take swift action to remove her from any committee that is in a place of responsibility at this critical time for New Wave church and the wider Christian community in Frenton.

Yours in his grip

A watchwoman.

I am sick to the stomach – in fact I thought I was going to throw up. Brian was kind, and when I explained what happened that night, he was lovely, and so understanding. Still boring, but nice . . .

Sleep is going to be a challenge.

TUESDAY, MAY 18th

Restless night, and woke up wishing that Mrs H was a dream. Sadly she is a living nightmare.

Had coffee with Laura this morning . I never cease to be amazed at her simple common sense. She's been consistently wise ever since I've known her, with the obvious exception of her madness with Dave. I still think she should have gone to the police – surely kidnapping is serious?

Anyway, she managed to convince Kristian to abandon his ridiculous music video idea. He's agreed, but since his new found 'passion' for the poor is the result of his catching 'the scent of destiny laid down by the Lord', as he describes it, I don't think we've heard the last of this.

When I told her about the latest dart from the dark (i.e. Mrs Hemming) she smiled. Laura never laughs *at* me: she smiles *with* me. That's a gift. Anyway, she said it was about time I realised that not everybody on the planet likes me, and I should stop being surprised by it. 'You've never had a proper relationship with Mrs Hemming – let's be honest – she's never liked you, nor you her. Why give her more power over you by fretting about her stupid letter writing? You explained what happened to Brian, and he said that as far as he was concerned, the matter was closed. So why not let it go? She's not worth it. Why give her space in your brain?'

Good old Laura. So very sensible. So very right. Most of the time.

Read a strange verse in the Bible tonight. It's where Samson is so angry with the Philistines that he rounds up three hundred foxes, ties their tails together, sets them alight and cuts them loose to wreak holy havoc in the Philistines' vineyards. That got me thinking. How long would it take to hunt down three hundred foxes? And to weave their tails together, while they're yelping and struggling to get away, while Samson ploughs on with his knot tying like an Old Testament boy scout? Revenge takes so much effort and energy. Perhaps that's why angry people sometimes have no space for anything else in their lives.

The trouble with feeling bitter is that it blights the good bits of life. After saying goodbye to Laura, I realised that we'd spent most of our time together talking about Mrs H.

And so we didn't laugh too much, and laughter is what we both need more of right now.

Thought of Mr Kyomo and his lovely laugh. I do hope they stay.

WEDNESDAY, MAY 19th

Great, incredible, wonderful news! Maybe my bad streak with men is over! After a series of disappointments, the dependable but predictable (and latterly hunky but now also married) James, worship-guru Kristian and wannabe-detective Aaron, I have finally met a man who seems – and this may be hard to believe – normal. He is from New Zealand, and by normal, I mean normal if most 'normal' men have a healthy colour rather than being pallid, and a decent body as well – not a pumped-up artificial looking muscle man, but just firm. And warm eyes. His name is Dex. Yes, Dex. Okay, perhaps the name is slightly canine, though it suits him, because he's relaxed – the opposite of uptight Aaron.

I picked Dex up on the beach. That's right, I went man hunting on the beach. I wasn't there solely for the purpose of picking up men, in fact I was there for a long walk along the sand, needing a breath of fresh air. Then I sat on my favourite bench on the Prom and watched the surfers man the waves or whatever it is surfers do. Apparently Frenton has some 'awesome swells.' I'm not entirely sure what that means but it looked rough out there.

When I spotted Dex I decided he must be from some foreign parts. The tan sealed the deal. There's no way you can get that tanned in Frenton, not even in the height of summer. Kristian occasionally sports an orange hue, but I know it comes from a bottle.

I decided that this guy was worth studying more closely, and I noticed a familiar design on his surfboard. It was an album cover from one of the few Christian bands I like, *Note For A Child*. They have this chilled out, soft vibe with poetic lyrics. Started getting excited at this point, and prayed, 'Please God, let him be a Christian, God, please let him be a Christian, please, please, please.' Then cynicism kicked in and I decided that he wouldn't be because the Universe is a dark and horrible place, waiting to do something nasty to me. Realised that I sounded exactly like Aaron. Decided the surfer dude must be a Christian. And what is more, I was going to find out.

I waited for what seemed like ages. Apparently the surf was particularly good that day, but I was determined. Finally he bounded out of the waves, strode up the beach, stuck his surfboard into the sand, unzipped his wetsuit and peeled it to his waist. I nearly died. But I was undeterred. In fact I was filled with even more resolve than before. How strange. Decided I would have to do this in the most casual way possible. So I stood up, looked like I was going to continue my walk along the Prom, and even tried to look mysterious. But the wind was blowing my hair in my face and I got sand in my left eye, so I was squinting. I hovered near him.

'Nice board', I eventually stuttered. He didn't hear me. Not a great start.

'Huh?'

'Nice board' I replied, shouting too loud, my squinting sand-filled eye probably making him think that I had a wink as a tic.

'Aw, thanks; yeah, my brother did it – he's a surfboard artist. They're one of my favourite bands. You heard of them?'

This was going well. I had managed to start up a conversation that was working. So I started talking about how much I loved the band, and what my favourite song was on their latest album, which was the same one as his favourite by the way (tell me that's not God!). Worried for a moment that he might not be a Christian, but a pagan who likes Christian music, but then he said one of the band members is related to someone in his church back home!

He was freezing after coming out of the water, and so was desperate for a warm drink, and invited me to join him for a hot chocolate. We ended up in a little cafe on the seafront having a chat about this, that and everything.

I know it sounds too good to be true, but Dex reminds me of Matt Damon – a younger version. I think it's the smile. His nose is large and bumpy, because it was broken when he got slapped in the face by his board in a surfing accident, but it is endearing. It gives his face character, in an Owen Wilson nose kind of way . . . I'm making him sound like a film star hybrid. Perhaps that's because he does look like a film star hybrid.

It turns out he's here for a while, doesn't know how long, staying with relatives in Frenton and seeing what the world has to offer him. He finished Uni in New Zealand (physical education degree) and then went on what was supposed to be a one year full-time discipleship course in Australia – but it didn't work out well at all, and he left after a few weeks. He said that the training was okay, but students were not supposed to ask questions about doctrine. Everyone else seemed so disciplined and certain, he didn't feel at ease. The crunch came when the course director told him that it was absolutely God's will that he stay for the whole year, and that he'd be rebelling against the Lord if he left, a betrayal of his calling. Dex saw the red light immediately. He didn't want to be part of something where questions were discouraged, and leaders told people what God's will was for them. He left the next day, phoned home and arranged to come to England for a while and stay with his relatives while he figures out what to do next.

I can't believe it. I have met a Christian surfer god on Frenton beach. And he's not any old kind of Christian – he's a full-on, going for it spiritual type, even if he is confused right now. I'm hopefully a full-on Christian too, and I live my life permanently confused. But after an hour of nattering together in the cafe (it was a three cups of hot chocolate conversation), he was 'sharing his heart' (a V term that works well in this context) with me. I think he is relieved to find someone around his age that he can talk to (okay, I'm four years older than him, but that's a detail), especially about his journey of faith.

'I'm struggling with the whole will of God thing', he said. 'I was certain it was God's will for me to go on the course, but it landed me in a real mess, and I'm glad I got out when I did. But I followed all the instructions from one of those books about guidance . . . you know, prayed a lot, talked to friends, consulted with the minister of our church, prayed that I'd get a place if it was right, felt peaceful about the decision . . . everything seemed to line up perfectly, I thought it'd be awesome . . . but it wasn't. So here I am, trying to decide what's next . . .'

Felt that it would be both premature and inappropriate to say that I was thrilled that Oz hadn't worked out, as it meant that he was here in Frenton and had met me, so kept quiet. His initial plan is to stay here for a month or so and then trek around Europe, but he likes Frenton and hopes to stick around longer.

Now that he's staying for a while, he's applying for a job in one of the bars on the seafront. He thinks Frenton is awesome, though Dex thinks a lot of things are awesome. I'm starting to think that more things are awesome too. He's catching. We watched the sun go down, which was awesome, and I asked him if it it was a disappointment as the sunsets in New Zealand must be much better, and he replied simply than a sunset is awesome everywhere and that we should hang out sometime again. I told him that I thought that would be awesome. He said he's surfing again tomorrow, if the weather's right. I promised to stop by, and we swopped mobile numbers.

Dex is so relaxed he made me feel relaxed tonight, which can be no bad thing. I feel like I have had a permanent knot of tension in me for ages. Knots would be more accurate. And think of it: we only met tonight, but I feel at ease with him already.

Called Nola (too late in the evening) and told her all about him. She says she's pleased, but seemed distracted. Perhaps I was wrong to call after ten. Or now they've moved I suppose they have other people to worry about.

FRIDAY, MAY 21st

Laura can't believe I picked up a surfer on the Prom! But she was thrilled for me when I chatted with her about Dex at work today.

Caught up with Dex on the same spot on the beach after work. Only had a few minutes, as he was packing his surf gear away. Turns out he has started going to a tiny little Baptist church outside Frenton, and they have a special speaker there tonight. Apparently the church wants to get more involved in the community and someone is coming to speak about God's heart for social justice. He asked if I wanted to go along with him, but I couldn't, had already arranged to have pizza with my mum. He probably goes to the church with the relatives he's lodging with anyway.

We're getting together tomorrow night for a drink at a little bar on the Prom round the corner from my flat. Is this a date, or what? Hope so.

Nice time with Mum, as usual, lots of news about the youth club. She seems happier.

Niggling worry about Aaron meant I finally texted *You ok?* yet again to him tonight. He texted back *Fine. You?* I wanted to reply, *Couldn't be better, I've met a gorgeous, normal man.* But it wouldn't be appropriate, of course.

SATURDAY, MAY 22nd

Spent the day cleaning the flat (okay, about two hours, the flat's not that big). Caught up with some admin from work this afternoon, and then met Dex for a drink.

I asked him how the justice meeting went, and his reply was interesting, because reading between the lines, it sounds like the speaker went on a rant, blamed right wing politics for every evil in the world, and tried to guilt everyone into action rather than inspiring them, which doesn't usually work. But Dex seemed reluctant to say anything negative about them. Says he met a few cynical people on the discipleship course, and he didn't want to become like them. He seems to want to give people the benefit of the doubt without kissing his brains goodbye. Speaking of kissing, I was pondering the subject a lot during our lovely time in the pub tonight. I spent forever (way too long, I think) telling Dex all about what happened to Dad, and he seemed moved and interested and didn't make me feel we needed to change the subject and talk about something else, which meant I talked for England. Dex nodded and listened; at one point, when I talked about Dad's memorial service and Hayley giving me a smile, I think I saw a stray tear in his eye. He's gorgeous, and sensitive with it. Bliss.

When it was time to go, he walked me home, and then thanked me for sharing some of my story with him. Then he kissed me on the cheek, said he'd phone, and would love to get together again soon. Can't wait. Can't sleep.

SUNDAY, MAY 23rd

Awoke with Dex on my mind, but then hurried to get ready for church as I'd slept through my alarm clock yet again.

As for church this morning, I don't think I have ever heard anything so boring in my life.

Old Mr Southey, who was evidently a preacher when Queen Victoria was an adolescent (okay, I exaggerate, but he is very old) – was the speaker. He did an incredibly long study of how the different parts of the Tabernacle point us to Jesus. I think it's called typology, or something like that. I got utterly lost somewhere between the candelabra and the horns of the altar (didn't know altars had horns). I think he had sixty-four different points to his sermon (sorry, exaggerating again, there were probably only seven or eight) and each point began with the same letter. I know these little alliteration devices preachers use are supposed to help us to remember what they've said, but it seems to me it makes everything sound predictable and Victorian.

Speaking of historic royalty, like young Victoria with her Albert, I am certainly besotted with my young (potential) suitor. Glad his name is Dex and not Albert though. Albert's not a great name for a surfer god.

The one benefit of Mr Southey's extended study in Jewish furniture was that it gave me an excuse to switch off and think about Dex. Who knew sermons were the new crush facilitators? In my fantasy, we were shipwrecked on a desert island. I was looking particularly lush in a pair of coconut shells and a grass skirt and Dex had to make do with a loin cloth. We'd spend our days spearing fish, climbing trees for nuts and berries and having blue lagoon moments in a rushing waterfall. I would get a golden bronze tan to match the one he has, would plait flowers into my hair and languish all day on the sand. And then rinse off in that blue lagoon again . . . all a convoluted fantasy birthed out of a drink shared in a pub and a kiss on the cheek.

My daydreaming was a welcome distraction, not only from the tabernacle tent pegs, but it also took my mind off the fact that I'm still missing Robert and Nola terribly. With the terrible preaching, it's hard not to think that

NWCF is going to suffer without them. Wondered briefly if I was going to join another church and then chided myself for being so shallow. Ask not what your church can do for you, but what you can do for your church. See? I could totally be in politics.

There was one slightly difficult moment when, in closing the service, Brian thanked Mr Southey for his 'word' and then, out of the blue, asked me if I would dismiss the meeting in prayer. Now the usual routine here is that you tell God what you've heard in the sermon, and ask for grace to live in the good of what you've learned. There's just one challenge with this: in order to pray what sounds like a kosher prayer, you would need to listen to the sermon in the first place. I think I did a reasonable job of bluffing though. My parting shot dismissal prayer went something like this:

O Lord, we thank you for the rich feast we have been provided this morning through the words Mr Southey has shared with us. Lord, there have been so many challenges (code for 'and I can't remember a single one of them'), so many blessings as we have dug deep into your word today. Thank you. Take us now into a new week, as not just hearers of your word, but doers also. (Here I blushed: just being a hearer would have been a good start on my part). Amen.

After the service ended Laura asked me if I was all right. Apparently I had gone slightly red during the service and she thought I might be coming down with something. At which I went bright red again and she gave me a knowing snicker. That girl knows me far too well.

Wondered for a moment if I'm ready to start a new relationship after Aaron and decided I don't care. This is the happiest I've been for a long time.

MONDAY, MAY 24th

Had sandwich lunch today with Laura in Marinabean, and she was upset. At first I was worried Dave had made another appearance, but I was wrong. Apparently Alpha didn't go so well last night.

She said she enjoyed the video teaching, and finds the posh West London accent of the presenter sexy, but it all went nightmarish when it got to the discussions around the tables. Some of the helpers were talking about the day they became Christians – and someone asked her about her 'day of enlightenment.' She'd said she couldn't remember a specific day, just that over the last few months she'd realised her need of God and had grown to love Jesus. Someone at the table got aggressive (they were probably trying to be helpful) and asked if she had specifically prayed 'the sinner's prayer.' Laura innocently said she didn't remember Jesus teaching people the sinner's prayer, but she prayed the Lord's prayer every day now. Didn't that count? Someone else jumped in and said what Laura was saying was great – there are loads of people, especially who've been raised in Christian homes, who either couldn't remember or didn't have a single day when they made a crisis decision; God had always been part of their lives, and what mattered was not how they came to faith, but they had come to faith anyway. That seemed to encourage her, but she still seemed concerned and worried.

It's interesting how such a capable person could be so thrown by a comment from a misguided but well-meaning person. We can be so wise when presented with other people's worries, but not have the answers for our own. She's also bothered about her night with Dave; she says she knows her thinking and morals are changing, and feels guilty about what happened, because she realises she now wants sex in a committed relationship with someone she's married to. She amazes me – some Christians take ages to figure that idea out, and some never do . . .

I so wanted to spend loads of time telling her more about Dex but realised there are occasions when we need to forget our 'exciting news' or even needs and focus on being there for others. Had a good chat, which helped her, I hope.

Dex phoned! Spent forever chatting with him tonight. Well, twenty minutes at least. Found myself telling him about amateur sleuth Aaron, and am worried because I told Dex that Aaron and I are no longer an item, which might make me sound too keen. But then again, I am keen. Really hope this goes somewhere. I think V and James get back tomorrow – can't wait to catch V up with my news of the heavenly surfer.

TUESDAY, MAY 25th

I was right. James and V are indeed back from honeymoon at last! Sounds like they had a marvellous time or, as V put it, 'heaven certainly kissed their conjugal union', which I think is a way of saying a good time was had by all. Bumped into them in Marinabean tonight. They do look deliriously happy together. V said they had made some useful 'contacts' for the gospel on honeymoon, which seems weird to me. I'm not sure I'd be running around trying to convert fellow holiday makers when I was supposed to be enjoying heaven's (hopefully) very frequently repeated kiss. They also went to church three times in Mexico too – which immediately made me feel guilty. I know James and V are dead keen to put Jesus first in their marriage, but I'm not sure that requires them to sit through a Bible study in Spanish when they're on honeymoon.

Apparently James got a stomach thingy from a dodgy taco, and V started to tell me the gross and explicit details, but I managed to change the subject by telling them about surf-god Dex. They seemed delighted, although V did wrinkle her nose when I confessed I'd found it difficult to concentrate on church last Sunday because I was busily thinking about Dex. V gave me a gentle but slightly condescending talkette about the potential power of lust. She didn't mean anything by it, but after we'd said goodbye and I headed for home it occurred to me that it was ironic for a couple who have returned from two weeks of divinely approved passion to give me, a single woman, a lecture about sexual constraint. And yes, I know there's a difference between lust and married passion. I don't need the lecture. Lovely to see them though. We've got another round of leadership interviews coming up soon, and I'm glad James and V will be there. Another late-into-the-night phone chat with my surfer. Awesome.

WEDNESDAY, MAY 26th

Woke up at 6am today and inexplicably decided to go jogging. I haven't been since I trained for the marathon, and as I found out straight after I'd finished that my father had been murdered, running lost its allure. Walking, yes, running, no. I stuck on my old training shorts and T-shirt that were a little bigger on me than before and decided to hit the Prom. It was a sunny morning, perfect for jogging, with a gentle breeze coming off the sea that helped to cool me down. I decided to jog all the way down the pier and stretch at the end. The sea was calm and beautiful, and there seemed to be hundreds of birds and seagulls about, freewheeling on the drifts. It felt good.

Got home and took a shower before deciding that I'd make a special effort for work and decided to suit up in light grey skirt and jacket set with a bright red blouse. Applied red lipstick. I don't know what it is about red lipstick but it always makes me feel good about myself. Suddenly realised I was feeling like the normal Helen Sloane. That I was making progress. Gone was the total reluctance to get out of bed in the mornings. Well, for today at least. I seem to be getting better, emotionally. Faith wise, I still have some serious issues to sort out with God, but it's funny how a good mood can make all those things fade into the background a little. And the thought of Dex helps, perhaps more than I know.

Got a text from Aaron, which said *Am mad with stocktaking at the shop. I'm fine xx.* Good. Don't know whether I should mention Dex to Aaron, having mentioned Aaron to Dex . . . no, that would be weird. Since when does a girl tell her ex-boyfriend she's got a new boyfriend, or at least someone who might become a boyfriend? Not a good idea.

Dex called and suggested we get coffee tomorrow. Hesitated for one millionth of a second and said yes. He's going for that job interview this evening.

Later

Dex called and he is now officially employed, starts tomorrow in fact. It's a casual part-time job working in a bar on the seafront called Fish Sticks. He said I should pop in sometime for a drink, but work means we won't be able to get that coffee we'd planned.

THURSDAY, MAY 27th

Training day at work – new procedures for interviewing potential foster parents. Am considering applying for a place on the selection board that approves fostering candidates, although it may be a bit early in my career to get a place. Would be a good experience and be great for my CV though.

Still trying to get some permanent care for Justin. The children's home are putting on the pressure. A tall order, unless I can find people who don't have a sense of smell.

Had a film evening with V tonight; it was good to get together just as the two of us again, and I don't think James would have been into the chick-flick we chose anyway. Talked about applying for the fostering panel with V, and she said she thought it was a great idea.

'I'm proud of you. You're making decisions that affect people's lives, and you're doing so as an agent of the kingdom of heaven. Perhaps, like Queen Esther, you have come to the kingdom for such a time as this.' Comments like these always bewilder me. Likening my being on a foster care panel to being a queen in an ancient Persian monarchy (and one who was a trafficked sex slave at that) is a stretch. Will apply though.

V headed home, and then Dex called during his break at work and asked about my day; I mentioned I'd been thinking about the panel application, and he said he thought it would be a great step forward for me – something new to get my teeth into. Such a wise surf god. Hoping to get into Fish Sticks to see him tomorrow.

FRIDAY, MAY 28th

Managed to get off work around 4pm so decided to go and say hello to Dex. I should have been nervous but there is something so casual about him, randomly showing up at his work (brand new workplace at that) doesn't seem like a big deal at all. I bet Dex randomly turns up all over the place back home in New Zealand. I said hi, propped myself up at the bar, ordered a lime and lemonade, and proceeded to either stare at the sea or watch men at work. Make that man at work. Dex. It was heaven. Stayed for an hour, and then things started to get busier, and I didn't want his employers to think he came complete with a stalker, so I headed home. Early night on the menu.

SATURDAY, MAY 29th

Just spent an afternoon with Laura – we seem to be getting close these days. We spent most of the time reminiscing about V's hilarious hen do, and I told her more about Dex. She said Dex sounds uncomplicated, which is exactly what I need right now in my life.

Hayley texted and asked if I would give her a lift to church again tomorrow. Mixed feelings about it – glad she wants to come, waste of time if she's still not interested, and complicated if she wants to keep coming. Will have to consult again at work about the professional challenges created by her wanting to go to the same church as me. Another enthralling conversation with Maeve on the cards. Yippee. Wanted to go and sit in Fish Sticks tonight but decided it would look too keen and freaky, so restrained myself. Only just.

SUNDAY, MAY 30th

Church was good this morning. Brian was speaking, and he was less boring than usual, although he disappeared down the alleyway of an illustration about molecules or something and never did get back on track. There was something about his steady voice which I found calming

– 121 –

rather than soporific. And it is good he knows so much about science and feels there's no contradiction between science and faith. He may be numbing at times, but he is thoughtful about his Christianity. It sounds odd, but it helps me to believe it because he believes it, if that makes any sense.

Have to confess I was so late, I ended up arriving five minutes into Brian's preach. I've got into an awful new habit of turning my alarm off in my sleep. Must either (a) get a louder one, or (b) put it across the other side of the room. Though the other day I did try (b) and woke up standing in the middle of my bedroom, holding my alarm. I must have made it across the room and half-way back before my senses kicked in and I woke up.

And then my lateness wasn't helped because I had to pick Hayley up again.

I wanted to ask her why she wanted to go to church again. Apart from a final two words of thanks after her last visit, she'd shown absolutely no interest in what happened during the service. And this time she was dressed in a short leather skirt and a low top showing everything she has, which isn't much, but it's more cleavage and thigh than is usually spotted around NWCF on a Sunday morning.

Spent most of the painfully silent drive to church praying the usher at the door would not be offended if Hayley treated his offer of a handshake like a rotting fish again, and he would look Hayley right in the eye when he greeted her. I got the vaguest impression that perhaps she was trying to test us, to see if we were going to show disapproval because she was wearing skimpy clothes, or if the men were going to leer. I shouldn't have worried, though. When we arrived, the usher remembered Hayley's name, was lovely enough to try the handshake, and seemed oblivious to her displayed charms. Hayley still didn't smile or speak (if grunting is not to be counted as legitimate conversation), but she did shake his hand. Small wonders.

Kristian bounded up, hugged me and said hello to Hayley, and she actually spoke: 'Hi.' He managed to keep his eyes front and high, but he stayed around too long. If he tries to get anywhere near Hayley, I will punctuate his next worship session by ritually disemboweling him, which might create a distraction. If he messes with her, I'll kill him. Oops. The 'killing' word is not one that works any more for me. Okay, I'll hurt him very badly.

He did do a good job with the worship, except that when he stepped onto the platform, he wasn't wearing any shoes (an act of identification with the poor broadly and the poor shoeless specifically), which looked odd, as he was wearing some smart trousers, so it didn't look casual or edgy – it looked like he'd forgotten to put his shoes on.

Overheard Dixie nattering with Kristian afterwards.

'Wot's with the shoeless routine then, Kris? Did you take 'em off because you were, like, on holy ground?'

Kristian looked a little bewildered.

'Well, Dixie, I am identifying with the poor of the world who cannot afford shoes.'

Dixie was having trouble with the concept of identification.

'Oh right love. Are you going to give your shoes to someone poor?'

Kristian shifted his feet.

'Er, no.'

'Right. Okay. Are you going to take the money you might normally use to buy shoes to help the poor?'

'No, I don't think so.'

'Are you planning on writing to the shoe companies to see if they could send some end of line shoes overseas? That would be lovely, wouldn't it?'

'I hadn't thought of that . . . erm, I might consider it . . . I'm not sure . . .'

'Oh well, darlin',' said Dixie without an ounce of guile, 'even though the poor shoeless are apparently gonna to stay that way, I'm sure they're very pleased and encouraged that you're – what is it – identifying with them. Very nice, love.'

Kristian looked confused as she walked away.

The Kyomos were there again. Mr Kyomo was chatting animatedly to Brian, and I overheard him thanking him for a great sermon. Looking good.

Hayley was quiet again during the drive home, but as we pulled up to her house, she turned and said, 'Thanks again.' Sped off before Mrs Tennant could greet me with yet another philosophical question about the origins of evil in the Universe. I've got enough of those questions to keep me going for a while.

James phoned this afternoon and they're short of helpers at Alpha tonight. He's asked me if I can step in. To be honest, am not excited about it, but said I'd do it. Robert and Nola used to say that often, being faithful to God is just about showing up when there's a need. So I guess I'll show up.

MONDAY, MAY 31st

Am surprised and delighted. I enjoyed Alpha last night, not least because Hayley showed up (church twice in one day – amazing) and all of her own accord. She didn't tell me yesterday morning that she planned to go. And she made her own way there, an effort (a walk and a bus ride), and her coming under her own steam makes it easier for me professionally. I wonder how she explained her sudden avid churchgoing to the God-hating Mrs Tennant; perhaps she didn't tell her where she was going.

Anyway, Hayley made an impression during the evening. There are about twenty or so 'new' people on the course, plus the Kyomos who are established Christians but are coming along as a way of getting to know people. Yes! They're staying!

As usual, James hosted the evening, but the main teaching, by DVD, was about sin and grace. Then came the 'now let's talk about it' part around the tables, during which Hayley was quiet. It was during the 'any questions' time at the end that she made her mark. She raised her hand, and shot James one of the bluntest questions, possibly in the history of Alpha. Probably in the history of humanity.

'Excuse me, does God know how many boys I've slept with?'

James coughed politely and looked as though he was trying not to blush – but how can you stop it?

'Well, yes, Hayley, he does know that. He knows how many hairs there are on our heads and . . .'

'I'm not bothered about him knowing about my hair. Does he know about that married bloke I hung around with for a while?'

'Yes, Hayley, he does. He knows the beginning from the end.'

Hayley looked very confused.

'Are you saying he knew what I was gonna do before I did it?'

James affirmed that, yes, indeed, the timeless God did have advance notice of her various (and apparently many) romps.

'Well, if he knew what was going to happen, why didn't he stop me from doing it, if it was so wrong? Especially as the married bloke was a complete . . .?'

James interrupted and launched into an extended monologue about how God created sex as a beautiful gift reserved for marriage. Unfortunately, as often happens with breathlessly thrilled newlyweds, he started talking about sex with too much enthusiasm.

At this point Brian, who was only there as prefect in charge of quiche distribution, jumped up and launched into an extended monologue about how God the engineer has created the mechanics of the Universe. Then he went on about the correlation between divine foreknowledge and human freewill, and predestination doesn't necessarily automatically imply predetermination . . .

It was soon apparent he'd lost everybody, so James chirped up with what he hoped would be a helpful comment.

'The truth is, Hayley, God sees you completely, and loves you completely.'

It went very quiet, and James probably thought normal service had been returned, and it was time to go home, when suddenly Hayley piped up again.

'If you're saying God sees me, and he sees everything, and we're talking about how many blokes I've had – are you saying . . . God watches? Bit weird, ain't it?'

Stupefied by the thought he had portrayed the God of the Universe as a voyeur, James spluttered and hesitated, at which point Brian jumped up again, and began to explain how the alternative to this involved God being a Deist Creator who effectively manufactured the Universe and then retreated to isolation and non-involvement, which would be incompatible with a God of infinite care whose plan before creation has always been to know and be in relationship to humanity, and how in a post-Edenic situation it was difficult to grasp . . .

James was about to invite Brian to sit down and be quiet for ever, when Hayley nodded, and said. 'Yeah. I think I get that. I think you're saying, he knows me, but he still likes me, eh?'

Brian smiled. 'That's exactly what I'm saying, Hayley.'

Hayley wasn't finished: 'Everything? Like, he knows, absolutely everything about me?"

Brian smiled patiently. 'Everything.'

And with that there was a final prayer, and the evening ended. Hayley took off quickly – I was going to offer her a lift home, but didn't get the chance.

James told me afterwards that although he thought Hayley was going to be a handful, she would be a breath of fresh air in what was normally a more restrained group.

We talked about the upcoming interviews for the leadership role. We've got another two people lined up for Tuesday night. The first is a lady who leads a medium-sized church in the north of England. What an irony. Why can't she stay up north, and Robert and Nola stay south with us? What's with all these chess moves anyway? And the second candidate is the assistant leader of what sounds like an uber congregation in London. It's only being going for five years, and apparently this chap feels it's time for him to branch out and become a senior leader himself, hence his application to us. Should be an interesting evening. Efficient Brian is going to email their CVs through. Decided I should take time to read them this time.

Good day at work. I think I might have found a potential home for Justin, but it's out of our district. Made contact with foster parents through the national database that is operated by local authorities, and they seem keen. I mentioned that there are some behavioural problems, including personal hygiene issues, but they are seasoned short term carers. I hate to say this, but if I can get Justin with them, then not only might they be able to help with his issues, but also another local authority will have the job of finding a permanent placement for him – and it will get him out of that children's home, which he hates.

Dex called tonight, apologised for being so busy, and said one of the staff at Fish Sticks has been off with flu, so they're asking him to work extra hours, and he wants to make a good impression, being so new in the job.

TUESDAY, JUNE 1st

Exhausted.

Busy day at work, including a case meeting where I mentioned Hayley's church attendance to Maeve. Her feeling is Hayley going to church independently of me makes it easier, but the situation does need to be carefully monitored so there are no inappropriate blurring of lines in the relationship. Got the impression Maeve is not too impressed with Hayley becoming a churchgoer. 'I do trust religious fanaticism will not be her next phase', she sniffed. She communicates a lot with a sniff.

She turned to go.

'There's one other issue I want to ask you about, if I may. I've been doing a lot of thinking lately, you know, about my experiences here and developing myself in my career in the future . . .'

That sniff again.

'Sure, sure. What exactly is it you want to discuss, please? I have a meeting starting three minutes from now . . .'

'I was thinking about applying for a place on the Foster Carers Selection Board. I think I could make a good contribution, and I understand there's a vacancy coming up, so . . .'

Two sniffs.

Maeve looked at me as if I were a first aid novice applying for a job as a brain surgeon.

'It might possibly be worth a conversation. Email me, please, and outline your reasons for thinking you might be a worthy candidate. I'll get back to you in due course.'

With that she was gone. What a warm, encouraging conversation that was. Not.

Quick coffee with Dex after work. He's enjoying the job but does find it hard at the end of the evening, when some people throw as much booze down their necks before closing time. 'I don't get the binge drinking thing at all, Helen', he said. 'There are a couple of regulars who are pleasant and friendly all evening, and then get off their heads in the last half-hour of the night, and turn angry and aggressive and end up throwing up outside – if we can get them outside in time. It doesn't look like fun to me – makes no sense.'

I agreed. I've seen enough mad behaviour due to binge drinking in my work.

'I think it's an image thing. Some people probably get off their heads because they want to look cool, yet when they're drunk, they look anything but.'

He nodded, but then looked a little uncomfortable, an unusual look for him.

'But doesn't image matter to everyone? I feel okay about the way I look – except for one thing.'

He paused, as if waiting for me to point out his imperfection.

'I absolutely hate my nose. It was fine before my surfing accident, but it's way too big . . . and . . . messed up.'

I told him I was very comfortable with the way he looks, which again may have been a tad keen.

Headed on to the church. Interviewing two candidates in one night is a bad idea, especially considering the stark differences between the two candidates we met tonight. The first was a lady (pretty obviously, as her name is Sue, and outside Johnny Cash's world, there aren't many boys named Sue).

She had a warm, open smile, and quite possibly the bluest eyes I have ever seen. I desperately wanted to ask her if they were real – not that she had false eyes of course, but those coloured contact lenses . . .

She came across as totally at ease with herself, and not eager to impress us at all. And I noticed that she used people's names when she talked to them, as if she realised that it matters. She replied well to our questions, and was particularly impressive – well, to me, anyway – answering a couple of them with 'I don't know.' Brian tried to get specific with her about six literal days of creation in Genesis versus a 'Did God create over millions of years?' discussion.

'What's your view about this?' he asked, in that slightly intense voice that he always uses when referring to anything that Dawkins might have an opinion about.

'I honestly don't know, because I wasn't there . . .'

Dixie tittered, but Sue hurried on, eager to not make light of Brian's question, or Brian himself for that matter.

'It's an important issue, Brian, but the way we view it isn't vital to faith. What matters is our conviction that God created. I realise that the debate is interesting, but I can't see the point of making something emphatic that there's some uncertainty about it in Scripture.'

Brian muttered something like 'First round to Dawkins' which was out of character for him; sometimes kind people get their warmth stolen by their need to crusade on issues. The rest of the conversation went well, and I decided I liked Sue very much. She was so . . . ordinary. She'd been raised in a Christian home, and had no startling Damascus Road fall-off-your-horse conversion story. She'd married the guy she first dated in their youth group (Colin, he's an English teacher), went to Bible college part-time, took up ministry, and she and Colin were sensing the need for a change, hence her interest in Frenton and us. Sometimes people use the word 'solid' as a description for others, which I think might be a code word for 'thick' , especially in the Christian world, where everyone is often stiflingly polite to the point of lying. But I think Sue is solid in the best way. V didn't smile much during the interview though. Mr S-B asked Sue a few questions about how well she manages people, and even put a couple of hypothetical situations to her to see how she would handle them. He seemed very happy with her answers.

After she left and we all had a chat, I realised things are getting tense in our committee now. Perhaps there's a sense of panic because Robert and Nola have been gone for a little while, and there was a bit of a stir when we turned down Mr. Bleasdale.

At first Brian was tight-lipped, but then V spoke up: 'I liked Sue a lot – but to be frank, I didn't sense great faith in her. To me, she comes across as a thoroughly decent plodder rather than a pioneer . . .'

I started to speak up, but V's comment seemed to spark Brian, and when he spoke, his nostrils flared, in a way that wasn't helpful with the regrowth of nasal hair. A vein in his forehead was pulsing away.

'I'm sorry, people' (I hate it when people say . . . 'people'), 'I thought Sue was a fine person too, but I absolutely, certainly, and emphatically could definitely not support a candidate who does not believe what the Bible says. It's the thin end of the wedge.'

James jumped in.

'That's not the issue, Brian. Sue does believe the Bible, but she wants to be sure about what the Bible is saying, rather than the ideas people create around it. To be fair, I'd guess that most of our congregation wouldn't hold to a literal six day view of creation.'

Brian wouldn't be dissuaded.

Then Mr S-B stepped in. He made a few warm remarks about respecting each other's views on non-essentials, and then suggested, 'I thought dear Sue was a good thinker and a thoughtful leader. I propose we ask her to come to preach for us and then the congregation can decide.'

The proposal was voted down; Dixie and Mr S-B voted in favour with me, but Brian and V voted against, and James abstained. He probably thought he couldn't clash too much with V, which was disappointing. Anyway, we need a clear majority to put someone before the congregation, so it seems Sue is not our woman. As we broke for a cup of tea and a 'comfort break' (another piece of

Christian jargon: apparently 'toilet' is a bad word) I wondered about our process. Did we believe God was getting his will done through our half-informed, patchy conversations and flawed interviews, hindered as they are by our likes, dislikes and prejudices? Hoped somehow, over the top of it all, God was sorting it all out and steering things. Decided not to ponder that one too much more or my head might explode.

The second candidate of the evening was a real turn off from the start. His name is Derek Jones, but he kept referring to himself as 'Pastor Jones', and we certainly got the hint we were required to call him *Pastor* from the start. The best way I can describe him is to say he seemed quietly angry. He did smile, but his smile was thin, even put on, a weak facade for his simmering soul. That was him: thin; in smile, in build and, seemingly, in joy.

He had dandruff on the shoulders of his blazer, and his trousers were a little too short for his legs, displaying lime green socks.

When we asked him about what critical issues he thought the church was facing today, he said the greatest lack in the church was holiness, and without holiness we wouldn't see God, and with it we'd see more of God and revival too. Things went downhill from there.

Not only did our holy man have a cold stare as well as the thin smile, he also carried a list in his head of off limit things no good Christian should do, including dancing (except in worship), going to the cinema (except to hand out Christian literature to the waiting crowds or to see *The Passion of the Christ*) and a host of other things that seem like a lot of harmless fun to me. I was stunned to know there were still people holding to these ideas in the church of today, and asked him if he thought his ideas were up to date. 'That's the problem, young lady' he said, using the term *young lady* with a tone of respect one might normally reserve for a slug. 'The church has imbibed the spirit of the age. We've become so desperate to be relevant, to fit in, we've become compromised. The salt has lost its savour and it's no longer useful for anything, except to be thrown out.'

I wanted to throw him out, right there and then. Helpfully, while everyone in the committee believes real holiness, is important, no one wants to descend into the legalistic dark ages. After we'd thanked him for coming, and he left, we had an extended conversation about non-biblical lists of prohibitions, Jesus' attitude to the Pharisees, and the nature of true holiness. Brian gave us an extensive little commentary about what he thought 'the spirit of the age' was, which was mostly about Dawkins. Then Dixie piped up and delivered the volley that made us all realise we didn't want to take things any further with Derek – I mean, Pastor Jones.

'E wouldn't be much fun, would 'e?'

I phoned Dex and he seemed interested; as he's not in our church I thought it was okay to tell him about our two candidates. We chatted about the sort of

Christianity that has lots of little rules, and he launched into this surfing analogy about how when we're doing what God wants us to do, it's like riding a wave, because he empowers us for it. Trying to follow human rules and regulations would be like trying to surf on a day when the sea is mirror flat. There would be no power for it, just frustration and a feeling you're going nowhere: no surfer would try it. I liked that. I like his voice too.

WEDNESDAY, JUNE 2nd

Can't believe it. Got a phone call from the college that Hayley's attending for her hairdressing course. Apparently everything has been going steadily down-hill, but it reached a new low today when she got some chemicals mixed up and dyed someone's hair bright yel-low. When she saw the results of her handiwork she flipped out and started lobbing dye all over the class-room, and threatened to stab her tutor in the eyes with a pair of scissors. That girl is one step forward, fifteen steps back. Will have to set up a case visit for tomorrow. Almost beside myself with joyous anticipation about seeing the most gorgeous Mrs Tennant again (yep, I know, I was being sarcastic there).

No contact with or from Dex, which I missed, but don't want to appear too keen. Laundry and ironing night. Dull.

Brian emailed the minutes of the meeting when we (hap-pily) declined the (unhappy) Rev Jones.

Hayley is back to being her old self. That girl infuriates me so much! It's like she doesn't care about anyone but herself – she wants what she wants and she wants it now. I don't care that she's asking questions at Alpha and 'livening up the proceedings.' There seems to be a real disconnect between all the talk about God and then the person she is when I go to visit her at home.

She seems to think she has a right to things, whether it's another pack of cigarettes, a bottle of cheap cider or some new gold hoop earrings. She can't see past the immediacy of now. It's like she doesn't believe she has a future for herself. She's so good at getting the things she wants but terrible at getting what she needs.

She wasn't even there when I arrived. Apparently she's got a boyfriend who she's been keeping very quiet about – been with him for a week or two, I think, but he lives in a mobile home in Duxford, which is a thirty minute bus ride from Frenton. Sometimes she goes out for the night and doesn't come back until the next day – and last night was one of those nights. Her boyfriend rejoices in the name of Blag, which may be the name his parents gave him, but I doubt it.

And so she ambled in twenty minutes late for our meeting, obviously unshowered and with an enormous love-bite on her neck that suggests she might have spent the night with Dracula. No apology for the lateness, not even a 'Hello.'

So began a frustrating conversation about her attitude to college. I tried to explain to her over and over the idea of long term benefits, hard work today means rewards tomorrow. But she seems so unwilling to believe it. She's started so well at the hairdressing course; I had to fight tooth and nail to get her in. But lately she either doesn't turn up, turns up late, turns up hungover or turns up abusive – to the staff and the students. Today she announced she was going to get herself knocked up and then she'd never have to work again. Imagining Hayley with a baby made my stomach turn. She'd probably leave it on a bus somewhere, or try and feed it turkey twizzlers. That said, perhaps motherhood would make her grow up. In some ways Hayley is one of the most grown up people I know, in the worst possible way. She can behave like a spoilt child but she's so street savvy and can size people up in seconds, probably to try to figure out what she can get out of them.

While I tried to reason with Hayley, both she and her aunt were sitting on the sofa; both puffing away on super kings, and staring at the *Ross Daley Show* on the television. I looked at some of the poor losers on television being taunted and lectured by Daley – I don't want life to be like that for Hayley. But what can I do if she wants that life for herself? If only she could pay attention long enough to put some effort in. She's a clever girl but she is full of a hopelessness that is destroying her.

In the end I gave up. Am worried about her vampire boyfriend though. And about the possibility of Hayley becoming a mother, if she's not careful – or perhaps she's calculated having a baby would benefit her.

Bright spot in an otherwise tough day: Dex called tonight and said he'd like to have lunch tomorrow. Yippee! Brian emailed another agenda for the leadership selection committee meeting tomorrow night.

Lord, please give Hayley vision about her future. Show her how different her life could be if she worked harder. Let her know she has worth. Amen.

FRIDAY, JUNE 4th

Fabulous lunch with Dex. He says he's enjoying Frenton but missing New Zealand and all his friends there. Had a terrible moment of panic that, just as we are starting to get closer, he's going to take off. And to ask for any reassurance would sound clingy. Praying he will see the light and stay, or just stay, even if no seeing any light is involved.

Yet another interview with the search committee tonight. Bumped into Mrs Kyomo on the way into the church. They've only been around for a few weeks, but they're on the cleaning rota already. Amazing. She showed me a picture of their son who still lives in Nigeria. Handsome looking chap. Found it difficult to concentrate on the interview, as was anxiously pondering the possibility of Dex disappearing out of my life.

Our latest candidate gave me a headache within seconds, and not because he was loud. On the contrary,

John is a softly spoken Kenyan man – and his speech was measured, deliberate, as if he was terrified a stray word might tumble out of his mouth and destroy the Universe. He's the opposite of me, I suppose, where much word tumbling is a part of my everyday life. First off, he was so utterly, terrifyingly certain about his faith. I don't mean confident, I mean certain with an unwavering, *I'm right, there's no compromise, no need for discussion, what's doubt anyway?* kind of certainty. But then, as the conversation went on, I realised why he was so measured with his words. It was because he believes they have creative power.

'We are agents of the kingdom', he said, 'and God calls us to create our own realities – blessing, financial prosperity, healing, whatever. And the way we do that is the same way God did it in Genesis: with words. God spoke, and created and so as we speak, we create in his name.'

By now I was feeling very uncomfortable.

'Proverbs tells us the power of life and death is in the tongue – so as we criticise people, we curse them, but as we speak wholeness and healing, so our words create those wonderful realities.'

I think John caught me off guard. I've seen these faith and prosperity preachers before on television – they are usually loud and flashy and aware of everything except that they've got very bad hair. John is none of those: he seems genuine, warm – but his ideas are the same as the crackpots on TV.

I thought about silently chanting a new mantra 'Let Dex fall in love with me and begin to hate the thought of going to New Zealand without me' over and over again, but then I realised John was spouting impressive sounding charismagic twaddle. Robert has preached on that Proverbs passage, and it's got nothing to do with harnessing creative energy by using words – it simply means we can help or hurt people by the way we speak. Having seen a few people verbally flattened by the nuclear verbal missiles that Mrs Hemming used to fire when she was around here (and still does with her occasional epistles, like the one about me coming out of Aaron's flat) I've seen the truth of the Proverbs statement at first hand.

But then something remarkable happened in the meeting. I'm not sure if John's softly spoken approach won people over, or whether there was a genuine fear that it would be racist not to nominate a black person for the 'trying out' preach, but somehow, John got a majority vote to move to the next step. I voted against, but I was the only one. V said we could do with some authority and faith around the church; James didn't say anything. Mr S-B seemed to think it was a fabulous idea to have a black leader, Brian was quiet, and even Dixie voted for him. Although she told me afterwards she couldn't understand any of his theology, she thought he was a thoroughly gorgeous looking man with a great body, and she'd seen enough racism in the East End, so she'd like to give him the benefit of the doubt. 'Besides', she said with a wink, 'if his sermons get boring or heretical, at least he's a looker.' I marvelled at the fact that ancient

Dixie still had an appreciation for eye-candy, and then, driving home, absentmindedly wondered how it works out when much older people get married. Do they still have sex, despite the huge potential for damage or death?

Anyway, it will be a few weeks before John can come to try out. Should be interesting, to say the least . . .

Brian emailed the minutes of the meeting, which helped me feel sleepy.

Night night.

SATURDAY, JUNE 5th

Spent a lovely hour in the seafront cafe with Dex. Have discovered one of the reasons I think he's absolutely lush: and it's not just due to his perfect body. It's as simple as this: he really listens. He is perhaps as good at listening as lovely Robert and Nola, whom I still miss every day.

I can see it in his eyes. Most people listen for only so long, and you get the impression they're biding their time before making another statement, especially when they give the game away by interrupting. Or sometimes they will listen, nod – and then turn what I've just said about me into an illustration of something that's going on in *their* lives. Even gorgeous V listens with a view to fixing me. In fact some of the more negative times I've had with her have been when she assumes this tilted head position that implies she's trying to listen to God as well as me (she would say she's trying to hear from God *for* me, but without sounding irreverent, at that moment I don't want to be part of a three way conversation. I want V's exclusive attention, without feeling she is on the phone to someone else – even God).

Dex has this fabulous habit of asking good questions, as though he's not satisfied with what I've told him, but wants to know more. Feel guilty after all I've just written about him – and I realise I hogged the conversation. All this stuff I'm saying about him being a good listener, I hope he thinks I am as well. He only talked briefly about what's going on with him this week (maybe he couldn't get a word in edgeways). He enjoys the little church he attends. Liking Dex a lot. Am hoping this is going some-where . . .

SUNDAY, JUNE 6th

Went to church this morning hoping for a dab of inspi-ration, only to come away with another example for my thesis that many Christian guys are mental, with the exception of one hunky New Zealander.

Kristian behaved very oddly with me in church today and I have finally figured out why. I walked in and spotted him, and despite my serious misgivings about him, decided to go up and hug him hello. I'm not sure what I was thinking; it seemed like the Christian thing to do. Since the grop-ing/unwelcome snog incident I've been trying to stay out of reach of his arm span at all times, but he happened to be standing in a circle with a few other people I wanted to hug and I couldn't very well miss him out, could I? So (and this is painful, I'm turning red remembering this) I reached out to hug him, whereupon he did a strange dance, a wiggle that resulted in him mysteriously appearing at my side and giving me a sideways hug. Needless to say, it was humiliating, and made me feel like I was carrying some terrible disease. For a split second, I had a flashback of bumping into Mrs Hemming when I came hurtling out of Aaron's flat: with her supernatural capacity for gossip, had news of that early morning encounter reached Kristian? Or perhaps Brian told Kris about the 'anonymous' letter Mrs Hemming had sent in? I felt irrationally unclean, even though nothing had happened that night. Guilt travels at lightning speed, and doesn't even need a reason. All this, because Kristian preferred a sideways hug.

I was angry. I'd decided to stay well away from him. The moment I finally forgive him for his bad treatment, he acts like he could catch something nasty from me. Felt slightly better when V swooped in to hug Kristian, and he reacted to her in exactly the same way. It would have been comical if it hadn't been so crass and insulting. So his response was not personal to me after all. Be still my beating, panicking heart.

V, being V, just asked Kris what he was up to. Did she smell?

'Well, it's like this. The Bible tells me that, as a man, I need to treat women in the church like sisters, with absolute purity.'

At this I coughed loudly and make a choking noise. There wasn't anything terribly pure about him lunging at me when he did.

'So I have felt led to take a "holiness" vow when it comes to women. I am not to touch them, speak to them alone or have any sort of intimate relationship with them. I won't even send women text messages.'

Talk about jumping onto the other end of the seesaw. He's gone from being a little too interested in women, to treating all women as though they are the agents of Satan, with the implication being that every single one of them (or at least in Frenton) is a Jezebel, hell-bent on seducing him. At least before he seemed to like women; apparently now we are all so sexually potent that even giving a girl a proper hug is inappropriate. He can't seem to get it right. We are either creatures to be pursued or to be feared. Can't he treat us like normal people?

Anyway, given up caring about what Kristian thinks or does. Just wish it didn't involve me. Makes me think of Dex, who when I said goodbye to him after we had sat talking in the cafe, gave me the warmest hug goodbye. Can't believe I used to think Kristian was some sort of sex god, now he looks like a petulant boy compared to Dex. Speaking of boys, all quiet from Aaron lately. Hope he's still alright.

MONDAY, JUNE 7th

Work (dull) and then long walk on Prom with Dex before his shift (delirious, delightful, delectable).

Another D-day. That would be Dex day! He started his shift later tonight, so after work we met and had another long stroll down the Prom. It feels so easy being around him. We can be in calm silence or natter on about any old thing. He was interested in how the search for the new leader of NWCF was going. We talked a bit more about 'Pastor Jones' with his comprehensive list of all the things you shouldn't do as a Christian, including dancing. We talked about legalism and why the church gets into it so easily. This might be a sweeping statement, but I wonder if people who feel like they can only be saved through following certain laws don't believe God loves them. Or that grace is somehow conditional. Dex agreed, but then said some people get into following mindless laws because they genuinely believe this is how to make God happy. They've been taught wrongly, but their motives are sincere. He's right, I'm sure. The point of grace (we concluded) is we are accepted though we are unacceptable. Quite a difficult sentence to fit all in your brain at the same time. But then I guess that's the point of paradoxes.

Dex explained that his Christian relatives (his mum's sister and her husband) with whom he is staying are lovely Christians but sometimes they focus more on what you should and shouldn't do, rather than enjoying their relationship with God. When they were younger they were both tearaways. He was a hippie guitar-playing wannabe folk singer and she was a chain-smoking peace protester, with a penchant for tying herself to railings. They were both avidly against the war in Vietnam, so they would often attend rallies and meetings – that's how they got involved in the church in the first place. Through the protests they met a few peace supporters who happened to be Christian, and the upshot of it all was they converted and started going to church. But it was there it all seemed to go wrong. The church they initially joined was fine, but after a few years they moved and ended up in a church that believed very strongly in heavy shepherding. They were taught a lot about being accountable to one another, which sounds like a good idea to me, but apparently this meant lots of confrontations, if one member of the church believed another was 'backsliding.' This was encouraged under the guise of 'community.' Apparently they would have forgiveness services where you would confront a fellow member of the congregation with whom you had a problem and ask for their forgiveness for your bitterness towards them. Sounds to me like a great excuse to tell someone you don't like very much that you have a problem with them.

I'm sure there would be a queue ten metres long in front of me if people had to ask my forgiveness for being annoyed at me. And Mr and Mrs Hemming would have a line stretching around the block, with people taking numbers from one of those machines they have at the meat counter in Sainsburys to manage the queues. The thought of the Hemmings made me want to tell Dex about our early morning meeting and her letter, but I'm not sure I'm ready to get into explaining the messy details of me and Aaron. Maybe later.

Anyway, I'm grateful Dex has a way of making me chill out. I stared at the sea some more and he told me about how close he feels to God when he's surfing.

He says the sheer joy of riding a wave, of looking at the sea and the sky join together, and the water beneath him is one of the most holiest things he has ever experienced. It's funny, because when I think about being close to God, I always think of it in context of prayer, or talking. Here Dex is experiencing God through doing something fun and beautiful. Maybe I should give this surfing a shot. Then maybe I'd have more excuses to spend time with Dex. I mentioned it to him and he immediately offered to take me out on the waves sometime. Oh gosh. Does that mean he'll have to see me in a bikini?

THURSDAY, JUNE 10th

It's going to happen. Dex called and asked if I wanted to try surfing with him on Saturday. Am thrilled and terrified.

FRIDAY, JUNE 11th

Tomorrow is my super sexy hot surf date with Dex, so today I went bikini shopping in anticipation. Though I have lost a little weight over the last few months, I am still no Kate Moss, more Kate Winslet circa *Titanic*. I went with V, for some morale support.

I have a confession to make. I've never bought a bikini before, I've always been a one-piece swimsuit girl with a preference for an underwired, extra supported sensible one from Marks and Spencer. Staring at the tiny string bikinis, I felt sick. They look like hankies with bits of string hanging from them. I think I'd need about four to even cover the vital bits, not to mention the extra coverage I'd like in other places. Ended up in the changing room with about twenty bikinis, trying to work out whether they were supposed to make me look like a porn star. I'm not used to wearing dental floss, and they look even more ridiculous because, of course, you have to keep your underwear on: hygienic, but not a great look.

And that's when it happened. I was struggling into one of the tiniest bikinis; it was pink, and had sparkles on it. It was the complete opposite of anything I would usually ever wear, which is probably what made me pick it out. Maybe I thought the pink sparkles would attract Dex. Somehow the bikinis I had already discarded had gathered themselves into a booby trap trip ball on the floor. I was peering round trying to get a good look at my derrière, (which had managed to swallow most of my knickers and the bikini bottom too) when I somehow got entangled, tried to regain my balance and ended up falling through the curtain and into the shop – right into a stand where I ended up sprawled on the floor. To her credit, V (who had been staring dreamily at some floaty kaftans) rushed to my rescue, bustling me back into the changing room. Once I'd retrieved the munched bikini pants from my bottom, I dressed quickly and we left for another shop.

Finally discovered a 1950s looking bikini which not only managed to hold everything in, but also covered enough flesh to be on the right side of respectable. Got home and discovered the top half of the pink sparkly bikini wedged in the leg of my jeans. I have officially become a shoplifter.

SATURDAY, JUNE 12th

I am now a surf goddess who has yet to master the art of actually standing up on a surfboard. Plus, the water was so cold, I chickened out after a while and sat on the beach wrapped in a towel. Most of the time was spent standing on a surfboard on the beach whilst Dex, blush, put his hands around my waist and told me to balance. However I seem to have been struck with clumsiness and kept accidentally, ahem, falling onto his arms. Oh dear.

My bikini shopping was a waste of time. My careful selection made only the briefest appearance before I had to squeeze into the wetsuit Dex brought along. He hired it from the local sports shop, and it was exactly the right size, which means he must have been checking out my figure . . . I think . . . not sure whether to be thrilled or sad Dex guessed my size rightly, but was delighted to see I fitted into a *medium*.

The surfing was spoiled when I saw a skinny figure dressed in black meandering down the beach with his hands thrust deep into his pockets staring moodily out into the ocean. Aaron, of course. He has a knack of turning up at the most inappropriate moments.

He spotted me and smiled and gave me a little wave, then shot Dex a curious dark stare and carried on his way. It was strange seeing the two of them at the same time. They couldn't be more different. Aaron was wrapped in a million layers, with his pale pointy face sticking out of his scarf, looking awkward and fragile, as if he was about to topple over. Dex, on the other hand, was perfectly at ease with himself, with the grace of an athlete. Dex looks larger than life. He makes me feel safe, whereas Aaron always made me feel slightly uneasy, as if I am permanently appointed to look after him.

When Dex and I were in the sea there was a moment when my surfboard whacked me on the back of the head and, disorientated, I breathed in a bit of water. Actually, it felt like half the ocean flooded my nostrils. Floundering beneath the sea, with water roaring up my nose, I suddenly felt Dex's arms around me. He hauled me up to the surface as if I was as light as a feather, although the water buoyancy must have helped, and stuck me on the surfboard where I could cough up the water (and expel some salty snot, yuk) at my own leisure. He didn't make a big deal out of it, but casually put his hand on my shoulder and asked if I was okay. I spluttered out 'Yes' and he grinned at me and said, 'Maybe that's enough for now. Let's get you back to the beach.'

We went to Fish Sticks and managed to get a couple of beers on the house. For some reason conversation got round to that strange prosperity preacher we interviewed for the church leadership, who is coming to preach for us soon. I think it would be terrible if he is appointed to NWCF. I said it would be funny if he didn't get the job, if everything came down to positive thinking. Maybe he was standing in front of a mirror right now chanting, '*I will get the leadership role at NWCF, I will get the leadership role at the NWCF.*'

This prosperity gospel stuff is strange. When we were talking about how these people say you should command God and demand what you want, Dex said, 'Sometimes what you ask for is not what you need.' Perhaps he's right, maybe we should trust in God to give us what is vital. Though, again, it's complicated. What about all the starving and sick people in the world? Is he giving them what they need? Invited Dex to dinner at my flat tomorrow, said I'd cook him up a typical Sunday roast. He said that would be awesome. Hope it will be.

SUNDAY, JUNE 13th

Church felt tense today. Nothing specific, but a few people didn't stay for the post-service cups of tea. And before the service started, I looked around the place and there were a few little groups of people standing around, muttering rather than talking. Not being able to find a leader is taking its toll. It's not that it's been a long time – I know of churches that have taken a year or two – literally – in their leadership selection. But the candidates that we've had seem to polarise opinions in the church, and there's a chilling sense that we're not as united as we were. Are any anonymous letters being sent to anyone else? Who knows?

Bright spot: Kristian has broken his new vow of not talking to a woman alone. Dixie is a mischievous old lady. After she'd heard about his vow involving evil womankind and had stopped laughing, she got a gleam in her eye. Apparently she got him alone using a series of compliments, little old lady comments and threats. I think she flirted with him thoroughly. I think it's a good thing Kristian is leaving womenfolk alone, I wish he'd get the balance right! Apparently he told Dixie that if he fasts from women for a year and a day, God will reward him with a perfect wife, and when that time comes, she will be the first woman he sees that day. (Sounds like the story of Jephthah in the Bible, who vowed to sacrifice the first person he saw: turned out it was his daughter). I think I'll make sure I'm out of the country.

On far more serious matters, Brian spoke to me at the end of church this morning. He had that look again – worried and furtive, and unfortunately his nasal hairs have grown back, which I found distracting. I think I knew from the anxious expression on his face that there had been another letter from Mrs Hemming – sorry, I mean, the watchwoman. Letters like hers have an especially debilitating effect on people, an ugly power. I was right. He handed me the note.

To the chairperson

Dear Brian

It is with great regret and sobriety that I write to you today. It gives me absolutely no pleasure (except the joy that comes from being obedient to the will of God) to tell you the Lord has recently revealed to me the terrible heart condition of New Wave church. I sense there has been a move afoot recently to completely reject God's clear call to total purity and holiness, and this has been a fatal step in the life of the church. Just as our Lord threatened to spit the Laodiceans out of his mouth, so I believe there is a final call to turn from wickedness. God is coming to judge his church, with the same terrible thoroughness that caused lying Ananias and Sapphira to fall down dead at the apostle's feet.

Embrace holiness. Embrace life. Turn before it is too late.

A faithful watchwoman.

I started to panic. How did she know so much information about our church and our committee? But what spooked me was her comments about holiness. Having turned Pastor Holier-than-God Jones down flat a few weeks ago, was it possible Mrs Hemming had heard from the Lord and now the sword of judgement truly was hovering over our church? It's a terrible thing to be told God might abandon you – even worse when there's an actual death threat implied by using such serious Scriptures as the Ananias and Sapphira incident. What did exactly Mrs Hemming mean when she said God had revealed the truth to her – was that a claim she had heard directly from God, or was it religious speak for the more likely truth that a shred of gossip had reached her? I tried to be as rational as I could, but I couldn't shake off the fear she might be speaking for God. Decided I couldn't begin to sort this out, so am going to try to forget it. And I told

Brian not to worry (even though I am). Dex is coming for dinner; don't want anything to spoil that, even a prophetic death-threat.

Dex will be here in half an hour, so why I have decided to write in my diary rather than man the various bubbling pots and pans on the stove, is beyond me. I guess I thought it would calm me down as I have been running round like a headless chicken for the past hour. Perhaps it's time for another shower, though I don't want to ruin my hair and make-up. The last time Dex saw me I was a surfer goddess (one with salty snot exploding from my nose) so I have decided he needs to see me in glamour puss mode. Have curled my hair and slathered on some red lipstick. Just checked mirror. Thought I had red lipstick on, but most of it had migrated to my chin.

Lipstick reapplied, chicken doing well in oven, vegetables chopped, waiting to go in at the last minute – don't want to serve him soggy vegetables. My splattered floor and walls are evidence I have whisked the Yorkshire pudding batter to within an inch of its life. Roast potatoes are in with the chicken and the cauliflower cheese is in too. Now all I need to do is one quick clean up and I'll be ready. Quick check to make sure my scruffy knickers have been removed from the radiators and I'm good to go. Wondering if I should light some candles or whether that will look too presumptuous? For all I know, he could just see me as a friend. Oh Lord, please don't let him see me as a friend. Maybe he takes all his friends surfing and rescues them from near death experiences.

I know. It wasn't a near death experience at all. However, in my head Dex has turned into some sort of bronzed Neptune, ploughing through the waves coming to my rescue. Oh no. Was that the doorbell?

Later

I have been kissed by a surf god. On a couch. With candles flickering in the background. After a glass of wine I decided I was brave enough to light the wicks, singeing my hair slightly (which created a brief but off-putting smell) but they seemed to have the desired effect. He said he loved the meal, which, although I say so myself, was very good indeed. We retired to the couch, and . . .

. . . his kisses were slow and leisurely, just like him. Heavenly! He's left now, he wanted to get up early for the dawn break, whatever that is. I should tidy up but I'm still basking in the glow of being kissed by a man who is one hundred percent normal. One point to me. Hallelujah! Awesome.

Got a text from Aaron just now. *Hope you're happy.* What does that mean? Is he genuinely saying he hopes I'm happy, or is this a sentence smothered with sarcasm, or even self-pity? That's the trouble with text and email; you can't see the person's face, or hear the tone of their voice. Anyway, decided pondering the nuances of Aaron's communication might spoil a perfect evening, so I texted back, *I am, thanks.* Nothing is going to rob me of tonight.

MONDAY, JUNE 14th

Most of the day spent absentmindedly thinking about kissing. What else matters? Happy, happy, happy, happy day. This evening Dex is working late so I stayed home and tried some Christian Celtic mediation. Apparently you sit in silence and try to open your mind up to God. Ended up thinking about what Dex looks like in a wetsuit. Tried again. It certainly was very peaceful. Didn't realise how loud my heart beats. Maybe I'll try it again sometime.

TUESDAY, JUNE 15th

Snatched a few minutes with Laura at work today, told her about the thrilling developments with Dex, and then took a huge risk in telling her about Mrs Hemming's letter.

'Listen, you rejected that preacher who was weird and banging on about holiness, not because you don't want to be holy, but because you don't want us to all get tied up in religious knots – what was that word you used for it?'

'Legalism', I said.

'Right. So look at the facts. Why would God want to judge you – and us – for walking away from legalism, when you told me that if there's one thing Jesus got angry about, it was the legalism of the Pharisees? What exactly are you worried about?'

It all seemed to make such sense when she said it like that, but last night I dreamt the most awful dreams about fire and demons and endless judgment, and then I met Jesus and he said, 'I'm sorry, Helen, I never knew you.' And he started laughing, a horrible laugh, totally unexpected, and then Mrs Hemming stepped up at his side, and she was laughing too, and I was being dragged off, and then I woke up.

I'm not sure what I believe about what I'm thinking here – but it seems possible for some Christians to bewitch others with their poisonous words. That prosperity preacher was wrong, but Proverbs is right – there is power of life and death in the tongue. And Mrs Hemming has a forked one.

Had dinner tonight with Dex, who is indeed lovely. Have never eaten buffalo before, but tonight I had the western burger, a bizarre looking concoction that came with a cowboy hat fashioned out of onion rings. Not exactly Michelangelo, but clever, I thought.

There was an awkward moment when I got the American flag that also came atop the burger stuck in my teeth. I'd tried to use it as an impromptu toothpick to get what felt like a quarter pound morsel out of the back of one of my molars. Unfortunately, it got stuck there, so there I am sitting with my boyfriend (the kisses on Sunday have surely confirmed that) with an American flag stuck out of my mouth. Dex laughed and started singing *The Star Spangled Banner* which made me laugh, and then I nearly choked on the flag. Not exactly cool. Dex has now seen me awash with snot and flying a flag from my mouth, and he still likes me.

It was a fun dinner, but even better was the conversation.

'What do you want to achieve with your life Helen? Do you think God has given you a sure sense of purpose?'

The question bought me up with a start. I've put destiny and dreaming on hold for the last eighteen months or so.

I thought for a while, and then surprised myself with the certainty of my answer:

'I think I do know, Dex. When I became a social worker, it wasn't because of a blinding flash of light or a booming voice – but I did have a compelling sense that this was what I wanted to do. I have some kids who can be dreadful to deal with, but in my worst moments, I come back to this idea that I can't get away from – this is exactly what God wants me to do. Although on days when Maeve gets sniffy, I'm not always happy. What about you?'

Dex paused for a moment. 'All I know for sure is that I'm open. I'd like to do something with people too, but have no clue how to work that out. I think I went to the discipleship training thinking that calling was something for "full time" Christian leadership. Since then, I've realised that we're all called to serve God – most in the workplace, a few in the church – but we're all called to make a difference wherever we find ourselves. So I'm not sure what that looks like, but I do know it's what I want. And I want to be with someone who feels the same way.'

Was jolted by that. What was he saying? That I might be that person? That I might not? What did make me very happy indeed was his full-on attitude towards God. Passionate without being weird.

Anyway, the date ended with a long delicious kiss. Even the previous consumption of the aforementioned onion rings didn't stop it from being lovely. Then went for a stroll along the Prom which ended up with some more luxurious kisses. Mmm.

WEDNESDAY, JUNE 16th

I can't believe it! Just returned from another case visit to Hayley's aunt's house, with the ghastly Mrs Tennant, which is why my hair stinks of cigarette smoke and I'm feel light headed. I swear you can get tipsy from being in the same room as that woman. The alcohol fumes coming from her could probably fuel the national grid.

Hayley's latest thing is trying to find herself. She's been hanging out more with Blag, her out of town boyfriend, which has meant more nights away, although Mrs Tennant doesn't seem to care. 'I'm only saying something because her room is such a state, and she does nothing to help around here. Always out on the tiles. Though, to tell the truth, I was like her when I was her age.' Imagining Mrs Tennant as an object of promiscuous desire is a stretch indeed.

But now Hayley has a major issue. Apparently there was a huge row last week between her and her parents, and it came out that the man she has always of thought as her dad isn't her real father. I think she was yelling at him, telling him what a worthless parent he was, and he retorted he hadn't done such a bad job, seeing as he's not her real dad at all. Seems he married Hayley's mum when Hayley was a few months old, and assumed the role of father – (in name, at least) until last week's blow up.

Now Hayley feels she can't properly find herself until she finds her real father, but how to track him down? Her insane, flat out barking-mad strategy to find him is to apply to go on the *Ross Daley Show*, the daytime glad-iatorial games of unfortunates who perform on demand for the red light.

Yep, I can't stand the man or his show. The worst part of it is the sanctimonious lectures he gives his guests. He humiliates them, brags he is in fact rescuing them, and then, even as they're convinced he's done them a big favour, rips into them with a dressing-down.

But Hayley has already called the number on the screen, had a phone interview with one of the researchers, and now they want her on the show as soon as possible. I don't think she knows exactly what she's getting herself into. She's convinced that once her real father finds out she is his daughter, he will collapse in tears and throw his arms lovingly around her. She's even hoping for a backlog of Christmas and birthday presents. What if he doesn't want anything to do with her? What if he's a nasty piece of work who will blight her already complicated existence?

She's asked her mum who her real dad is, but she doesn't seem to be telling – or maybe isn't sure. It seems it's a choice between at least three different men. But seeing as Hayley's mother spent most of her teenage years drunk, had Hayley when she was fifteen, and the conception happened when she was high on glue and drunk on cheap cider, Hayley's father could be one of many.

Anyway, Hayley wants the three 'suspect' men to appear on the show, so she can discover which one is her father, though probably not before Ross Daley has whipped them all up into an emotional mess. The DNA tests are expensive, so the only way Hayley can find out her father's identity is through the show, they pay for all the tests and offer expenses. If they've got any sense, they won't agree to appear – and then there will be no show. Hayley also seems to think this will make her famous.

'If that Jade Goody bird could do it, why can't I?', she said when I suggested that fame at any price in general and appearing on the show in particular might not be the best idea.

'I'll be famous. When Chantelle down the road went on it, people bought her drinks in the pub for weeks. She was trying to find out who her baby's dad was as well. It turned out to be Danny after all, but you never know.

Chantelle always loses her memory when she's been on the juice.'

Later I broke the rules and told Dex about Hayley's decision, without naming Hayley of course. He'd never heard of Ross Daley, so I explained he's a talk-show host, notorious for offering his aggressive opinions about his guests. Putting a girl of seventeen on national television and ridiculing her is too much. No one deserves that. And Hayley had been showing some progress over the last few months, even if her hairdressing training is currently in meltdown. But I think she still wants to be a qualified hairdresser, even if she's spoiling everything with her tantrums at the moment. When I was at the house today she offered to give my split ends a trim. I refused, too quickly, maybe I should have let her do it, as a form of encouragement, though I happened to notice her aunt's hair looked uneven. I asked Hayley about it and she confided that she thought she'd have a little practice on Mrs Tennant while she was passed out cold on the sofa.

I wonder if there's any way I can stop her appearing on the show, but apparently it's her legal right to do as she pleases, now she's seventeen. For safety's sake the Daley people want her aunt (as guardian) to sign a letter of permission and the lovely Mrs Tennant has no objections, so that's that.

Lord, please protect Hayley. I know she can be difficult, but is this a good idea for her? Please protect her from further harm and make sure this isn't one more thing that damages her. Amen.

Went into work today and asked Maeve if there was anything I could do to stop Hayley appearing on the *Ross Daley Show* next week. There is nothing, she replied in one sentence and then marched off. My last hope was that one, if not all, of the potential fathers would refuse to appear. But a phone call this morning to Hayley revealed that apparently they're all going – they're all convinced they're not the father and want to be vindicated. I think they're worried Hayley might turn up at their houses and ask for cash, claiming she's their daughter, and they want to stop this happening.

I tried to dissuade Hayley again but she is so stubborn. I can only pray that whatever happens, she won't be too hurt. I asked her if she wanted some company when she goes on the show and, to my surprise, she said yes. I am supposed to see Dex that day, but I'll have to cancel. Hayley is not only the bane of my life but also the bane of my love life! That said, I do have deep affection for her. I've been her social worker for a long time, and though most of the time she seems about as grateful as a lamb in a slaughterhouse, I have seen some small improvements. Make that tiny.

Tonight I went for a walk on the beach with Dex to watch the sunset and he whipped a blanket, a bottle of rosé and some strawberries out of his backpack. Points out of ten, eleven million! It's so easy to be quiet with him, not an uncomfortable silence you feel you need to fill, but a gentle silence of two people enjoying each other's company. He put his arm around me as he noticed I was chilly and before I knew it he was giving me strawberry-tasting kisses. I felt like I was in a romantic film, I thought at any moment the director would pop up from nowhere and shout *Cut!* But this wasn't a film, this was my life. Being with him is such a welcome relief from all the challenges of Hayley at the moment.

FRIDAY, JUNE 18th

Brian called to say that yet another letter has arrived from the wicked witch. Sorry, I know I shouldn't use that kind of language to describe Mrs Hemming, but this is getting ugly. Brian is exhausted, and the atmosphere in the church is getting more and more sour. There seems to be so much whispering and a tense awkwardness, which is so sad when you think how close we have all been in the past.

We have John, the mighty man of faith and power for the hour, coming this weekend to do the trial preach. He's asked for accommodation, not only for his wife and three kids, but for two 'assistants' from his church too. Apparently leaders like John never travel any-where without these volunteer helpers. I think he called them his 'armour bearers.' They sound like minders packing Bibles to me. But apparently Mrs Hemming has found out he and his entourage are heading towards town.

Brian had scanned the latest letter in and forwarded it to me with *Can you believe this?* in the email header.

Dear Brian

I wrote to you recently as a deeply concerned fellow member of the body of Christ concerning (a) unsuitable members of your committee and then (b) the matter of holiness being a terrible casualty in the church there. I am grieved you have not seen fit to react appropriately to (a) although, of course, your response to (b) is an ongoing matter and is, I suppose, between you and God.

But I write today as I am very worried about the further erosion of the New Wave Christian Fellowship there due to the infiltration of false doctrine, namely faith and prosperity teaching of the kind often propagated by television evangelists. Whilst I have a great affection for sound Christian television programming (we view no secular material in our home) I have to say that this teaching is largely deceptive and tends to focus on materialism in a way that reduces the gospel to a good investment package. It has also been my unfortunate experience to see Christians hoodwinked into believing that denying clear medical symptoms of sickness is an act of faith; I gather the terminology used here is 'positive confession' whereas in my experience this foolishness has been nothing more than a descent into total unreality. Has not the New Wave Christian Fellowship heaped up her sins before the nostrils of the Lord as she has continued to meander in ways of such folly?

I call upon you, as a trusted person in the church, to call the entire congregation away from this madness.

And one evidence of this turning would be the cancellation of the false prophet who is coming as a candidate at the church this weekend.

Yours ever vigilant

A watchwoman.

As I read the letter through, I knew two things with absolute certainty. Mrs Hemming was right sometimes. She was on the mark with her analysis of this prosperity stuff, although her language, tone, unsigned letter, shrill threats – all of these were way out of line. But I realised people who are wrong are not always wrong, any more than people who are often right are therefore always right.

And then it occurred to me, and I wondered why I hadn't seen it before, Mrs Hemming didn't have a direct line of revelation from God at all, in this or any other of her spiteful notes. But she did have a hot line to somebody. Mrs Hemming had a mole in our midst, who was telling her the details of our painful journey in a way only an insider could. The question is – who?

SATURDAY, JUNE 19th

Saw Mum today. I mentioned I had bought some nice things for the flat and she seemed to jump on the bandwagon and decided to take me shopping: 'There's nothing like new sheets to make you feel better', which makes sense to me, even if it doesn't sound like something out of the book of Proverbs. We chose some very pretty white and light blue sheets and pillowcases, and Mum bought me a couple of towels to go with them.

I asked her if it was strange sleeping alone now Dad has gone. She replied it was the hardest thing she'd had to do. In the day time she could pretend he'd gone out, or was at work, but at night, when she'd reach across to his side of the bed, she'd find it empty. Those were the nights she felt were impossible to bear. She'd confessed she'd even started shoving some pillows down his side of the bed. I told her she could sleep round my flat any time, but she said no, she might as well get used to it sooner rather than later, considering she doesn't think he's coming back any time soon. She gave a small laugh, and said, 'Anyway – he's probably having a great time with Jesus.' Didn't know what to say to that.

Got home and put my new sheets on the bed and tidied up the flat a little. It looks a lot more homely than it did before. Time for bed. Lovely sheets. Lovely Mum.

Dex phoned and asked if I wanted to go for a bike ride, which I felt might be difficult, seeing I don't have a bike. He's working tonight but wanted to spend a hour or so with me before he starts his shift, so he showed up with a couple of bikes he rented from a place on the Prom. Lovely time, which wasn't even ruined when I tried to ride the bike up a pavement that was too high, and nearly flew over the handlebars when my machine stopped and I didn't.

SUNDAY, JUNE 20th

What an absolute nightmare of a morning. I am so angry and confused.

John showed up with a beautiful family and two Bible toters. He was around as the congregation arrived, shaking hands, smiling, but the armour bearers were never far away. I decided to go up to one of them and say hello. His name was Terry, and he told me he'd been a Christian for about ten years, since then had always been a member of John's church in London and he enjoyed being an AB (armour bearer). He explained the meaning of the term, although I confess I didn't think much of his explanation. Apparently in Old Testament times warrior kings like Saul would have servants who went into battle at their side, carrying weapons and spare armour, and doing anything the king wanted them to do. Their job was simply to be at his bidding. And that's what these ABs do for the leaders in this church in London. Do they need a glass of water, or their Bible carrying? Is someone from the congregation being too intrusive? Does the great man need a 'catcher' when he prays for people to be healed? What about driving the car to and from preaching venues? Enter the ABs.

I was amazed. If this was the kind of VIP treatment the assistant minister of this church got, what kind of adulation was there for the head honcho? As I listened to Terry talking, I had to work hard to stifle a giggle, because it all seemed very silly, but it was obvious he takes it all seriously, considers his position to be a high honour, and also feels he is serving God as he serves his leaders. But when John suddenly called Terry to his side and told him, without so much as a 'please', to take his Bible to the lectern at the front, I felt angry that this lovely man was being used in this way.

The service began with Brian welcoming John, and his family (the ABs didn't get a mention, I think at their request, they're supposed to stay humble and anonymous) and then the worship team did a reasonable job, even though it was led by Kristian. Thankfully, I think he has retired his bleeding poor song (at least for now) so we were spared that agony. Mr S-B came up and led us all in a very erudite prayer, and then handed the service over to John – who immediately asked Kristian to come back to the platform. Scratch that. He *told* Kristian to come back to the platform.

'The worship was good enough, people of God, but there was no breakthrough', he said quietly, but firmly. 'We need to push through, refuse to back off, until we see a crack in the enemy's lines. Kristian, lead us again.'

It was awful. Kristian chose the fastest song he could find, something about stamping on the serpent's head, and the singing was punctuated with John holding the microphone very close and speaking out exhortative little sentences to whip us in a greater lather. 'Yes, yes, push through, God is good. Oh yes, oh yes, oh yes!'

I hated it. The only relief was the sight of Dixie clapping and hopping around at the back. She was obviously enjoying John, the lovely hunk, but she was also laughing. Afterwards she told me why. 'I thought the idea of singing until we discover the enemy's crack sounds like a lot of fun, darlin',' she said.

Anyway, we sang and sang until even Kristian looked tired of playing (which I've never seen happen before) and then John moved into his sermon. Again, there was no shouting, no histrionics, but a string of Scriptures thrown together that told us we have authority over everything and we'd better get on and use it. I felt wiped out by the end of it. I looked around the congregation; the Kyomos were not looking happy. This was the first time I have seen Grace's face without a hint of a smile. Even Mr Kyomo looked stern.

Then I looked over at the Murphys, a newer couple who had experienced a stillbirth last year – did that happen because they didn't have authority? And there's Alan, who always sits alone at the back. He's still heartbroken because he lost his wife Jane to leukemia two years ago – and then his only child got pneumonia and died. Now he's alone. I studied his face as John spoke. Agony seemed to be etched even deeper there. And then I thought, of course, about my own poor broken bloodied Daddy dying on a fag strewn street; did someone forget to take authority? While John was speaking, the ABs nodded. At one point he told a vaguely funny story, and poor Terry and his fellow AB laughed too loudly, because this gag was only worth a small giggle, and was a million miles away from the belly laugh they gave it.

John ended the sermon, closed his Bible, and I knew we were not done. He asked if there were any who needed healing, and called them to come forward to be anointed with oil. I watched as he prayed with each one, never closing his eyes, as if he could see what no one else could, and then one by one they fell to the ground, caught by the ABs with practised grace. Even from where I was standing, I could see he was giving them a hefty push to help them on their way, and I felt guilty at being part of this Godless theatre. Dixie went forward, although she later confessed there was nothing wrong with her, but thought the laying on of John's hands was nice.

I couldn't wait for it to be over. I was glad Laura wasn't there: she's fighting a cold, probably due to an acute shortage of authority. But here's the bit I don't get. Brian has struggled with a perforated eardrum for years. He went forward for prayer, and John smeared olive oil on so thick I thought he was prepping Brian's hearing gear for a barbecue. Then John put his fingers in Brian's ears, and said, 'In Jesus' Name!' and, after a pause, asked, 'How is it, brother?'

Now Brian's no mug. He likes everything to be kosher – he may be boring but he's thorough. He was born to be a physics teacher. I couldn't believe it, because he started crying. 'The ringing in my ears has stopped. And the pain has gone', he sobbed. I've never seen Brian cry before.

People started clapping, and V chose the moment to do a warrior queen dance of victory at the front of the church. Looking around, others were obviously sharing my concerns about what was going on. Some looked angry. Some looked confused. Brian's announcement prompted John to insist we sing yet another song, and then Brian thanked John (very enthusiastically) for coming, and announced that immediately following the service the membership meeting would convene to vote on the proposal that John become our new minister.

Thirty minutes later, as Brian called the meeting to order, you could still feel the strange mixture of confusion and excitement in the air. John, his family and the ABs had gone. Now we were supposed to vote. And that's when Brian did something that enables me to forgive him for his tediousness, and be grateful for him forever. He proposed that the meeting be adjourned for four days. Having announced we were going to vote, he'd had a few conversations in the half hour following the service, and he realised there were lots of concerns that needed to be thought about before the church could be pressed for a decision.

'We've had an interesting time here this morning, which some of you are thrilled about.' V and Dixie were beaming. 'And I have very definitely experienced something I have never encountered before. Obviously I will need a doctor to confirm it, but I believe that this morning, I have been healed of a long term painful condition.' Lots of clapping and some cheering, but still some gloomy looks prevailed.

Brian continued. 'I've talked to a few of you in the last few minutes, and I realise now that this atmosphere is not one in which we should make a decision as important as the selection of our new leader. Let's calm down, and reflect. Let's pray. And let's hold an all-membership meeting this coming Friday, and vote on John then.'

Later, just about everyone had left, and I was still sitting there, pondering. Grace Kyomo came over and sat down next to me. She'd been washing up tea cups. I desperately wanted to ask her what she thought of the service, but was worried, either that she loved it too much, or hated it too much, and would be offended by our conversation whichever way it went. I caught her frown earlier – but was this because she disapproved of John, or was picking up on the very mixed response from the congregation? So I decided to jump in with both feet.

'Grace, what do you think about this morning? I'm angry, confused, wanting to believe something good happened here, desperate to believe something flaky happened here too . . . what do you think?'

She smiled that amazing smile and paused. Must learn to do that. 'I think you're absolutely right about the good and the flaky being all mixed up this morning. This kind of message isn't new to us. We had a large group in our previous London church that was into it in a big way, and some very well known preachers have visited Nigeria with their message of prosperity, which, as you can imagine, is always well received. Why wouldn't it be? When a man flies in, in a private jet, and announces that terrible diseases are going to be banished, and people are going to prosper, who wouldn't want to hear that? But the trouble is, that theology doesn't work in Africa, and if theology doesn't work internationally, if it doesn't work wherever it is preached, then it isn't true.'

I was impressed. 'But Brian was healed today, you saw it. God did that, or so it seems. Do you think Brian was misguided?'

That pause again. 'No', she answered quietly. 'I believe it's entirely possible – probable actually – that Brian was instantly healed, and God did it.'

Now I was even more bewildered.

'But how come God shows up in the middle of a carnival like this morning and does good things? Isn't that going to confuse people? Isn't a divine appearance an endorsement?'

Grace smiled again. 'That's where we go wrong Helen. We want to box things up and label them "good" or "bad" – "of God" or "not of God." But it doesn't work that way. God is constantly showing up in the very mixed bags that are our lives, every day. In the midst of our goodness and badness, faith and doubt, insight and stupidity, God walks through it all. He arrives in the mess, and works in our untidy lives. His being there doesn't endorse everything we do; but when he catches the scent of a hungry heart, he comes running. It's confusing, but it's called grace.'

I drove home, and remembered Laura had said something similar about V's eccentricities.

Am so grateful the Kyomos have arrived on the chaotic scene of NWCF at the moment.

Got a text just now from V, which was predictable and worrying.

Prse Gd 4 the pwr we saw 2day.

Decided in desperation to phone Robert and Nola. Robert was lovely, and let me talk – but then (perhaps wisely) said it wouldn't be a good idea for him to comment too much on the leadership selection process. Hard though it is, he needed to let the committee and the church do their job without his interference. And then, with a laugh, he said 'Hope you appoint someone sane, though . . .' I got his drift immediately.

Nola came on the phone and said she was sorry if she sounded distant last time I called: she had been battling a migraine. Felt bad about thinking she had other fish to fry, and cared any less about me. 'If you're suffering with migraines, you need to come back to NWCF, Nola.' I said. 'We're a miracle church now.' A little naughty.

Sent V a text back that will hopefully provoke a good conversation, and summed up my thoughts about the 'power' we experienced today (and, it seems, my life at the moment). It simply said *I wonder*.

Texted Dex – he's working the late shift. Just said *Please pray. Am confused about faith. Talk soon. Hx.*

Dear Lord, I'm confused about all this faith stuff. Please talk to me soon about it. Amen.

MONDAY, JUNE 21st

Perhaps I'm all stoked up by the events of yesterday, but I don't think I've ever shouted at anyone so loudly in my life. Today I have been recorded on a national television show yelling at a famous television host and despite being in a small pit of red hot embarrassment, I feel good about myself. Someone had to say something, and instead of just standing there, at least I stood up for what I believed in.

Accompanying Hayley to the *Ross Daley Show* in London meant driving her there. Apparently she wanted to keep the money they'd given her for a train ticket for other purposes. I picked up a sleepy Hayley at 11am, which apparently, according to her reaction to the daylight, felt more like 4am to her. I think she'd done another all-nighter with her boyfriend Blag. No evidence of vampire activity, though, at least none that's visible.

'This had better be worth it' she muttered to herself as she got in the car, as if her appearance on the show was my idea and for my benefit, when I've been desperately trying to convince her she shouldn't go through with it. Then she plugged her iPod into my CD player and blasted rap music at a volume to make the Rolling Stones' ears bleed.

She had dressed up. Or at least she seemed to be wearing more bling than normal and had her best *Juicy*

Couture tracksuit on, in pink velour of course. Her hair was so scraped back she looked Japanese. I don't get her. One minute she's on an Alpha course giving James a run for his money, and the next she's in my car talking about how much ganja she smoked the night before at her boyfriend's place and how Wayne did Lydia round the back of the bins. Effing and blinding, calling me a stuck-up bitch when I wouldn't let her smoke in my car, she even tried to pilfer the change I keep in my ashtray for parking. I think nervousness was fuelling her nastiness.

Once we arrived at the studio I received a few suspicious glares from the production team who swooped on Hayley, and took her off for various meetings, briefs and psychological evaluations which were supposed in ten minutes to prepare her to receive the answer to a life-altering question – the identity of her dad. She was kept well away from the unholy trinity of possible fathers, and not given one clue as to who it could be: that would spoil the tension of the show itself. This struck me as being particularly nasty. These people knew intimate information that could potentially change a young girl's life forever – and yet they wouldn't tell. They were wait-ing to spring it on her in a studio full of people, under bright lights, through a TV host who may or may not decide whether to shout at her. Of course he did shout at her. That's Ross Daley's hallmark.

And so to the show. Hayley was the first guest – there were four in total, and all were looking for their real fathers. Ross didn't waste any time, but got right down to the heart of the matter, asking why she wanted to find her real dad. Hayley said (all too honestly) she wanted him to give her some money to make up for all the years he'd been absent. That triggered an early rebuke from the great Ross: he seemed appalled, as if Hayley was a disgraceful gold-digger (rich coming from a man who makes a very good living using people for money). Then he asked what she'd do with the cash and her ridiculous reply showed she was trying to be outrageous – shock tactics to grab at the possibility of fame. 'I'll do whatever I want with it – spend it on booze and blow if I like.'

Ross let her have it with both barrels. He seemed oblivious to the fact that she was playing up to the moment, wanting to be the bad girl for the cameras. I was standing in the wings of the set, so filled with apprehension that I was actually shaking. I didn't want this to go on but I could hardly fling myself in front of the cameras. This was Hayley's decision and I had no control over it.

But all that changed. When they brought on the three sheepish potential fathers, I got angry. This was not something that should be happening on national TV in front of a live audience who had already made their minds up about the guests. Sneering and laughing at Hayley in equal measures, Ross went through his usual rigmarole of shouting at each of the 'fathers', asking why they hadn't come forward for a DNA test before. One of them, Steve, who had terrible teeth and skin to match (and who would have been significantly older than Hayley's mother when she got pregnant at fifteen) got bellowed at for being a paedophile, but at least Hayley was left alone for a while. Steve didn't look too fazed, and just gave the camera a bleary-eyed smile. I wondered what he was on.

Jim, the second dad, looked like he didn't belong on the show at all. In a studio where dreadful tattoos and piercings were plentiful, Jim looked like a Mormon missionary, which I'm sure he was not. Apparently he had managed to do an Open University course and had a good job at a bank. If he turned out to be Hayley's dad, she might have hit the jackpot.

Mike, the third of the 'fathers' suddenly erupted at Ross, 'Look at 'er. Look at the state of 'er. Would you want that for a daughter? Not me, pal. I hope to God she's not mine. If she is, then I'll give 'er some cash, but that's all she's getting out of me.'

And then he turned and faced Hayley.

'You don't get it, do yer? It doesn't matter what the test says. I don't care if it proves I am your father. I'll never be your dad, because I don't want you. I might happen to be the sperm donor that made you 'appen. That's all.'

Through the tirade Hayley's face was set like stone. But then she looked over at me – and I could see there was a faint gleam in her eyes, as if she were holding back tears. Suddenly all of her cockiness had gone. Even Ross looked stunned by the viciousness of what was being said to her, but it didn't take long for him to recover.

'How does that little speech make you feel, Hayley?', he asked, keen to exploit the awful moment. She sat there, saying nothing, eyes filling up.

Ross waited, milking the dramatic silence, and then, at last, a black T-shirted production assistant handed him an envelope containing the DNA results. Deliberately, Ross opened the envelope, laughed, turned to Hayley and then dropped the bomb.

'Here we go, Hayley, the news you've been waiting for.'

Then he turned to face each of the 'dads' in turn.

'Steve . . . the results are in . . . and you are *not* Hayley's father!'

At first Steve looked impassive, as if he couldn't care less one way or the other. Then he smiled.

'Jim, I have your DNA test result too . . . and you are *not* this girl's father.'

Jim nodded, relieved, and turned to mutter something to Steve. Both were now off the hook.

It was Mike's turn. Mike the sperm donor, the nasty piece of work who felt able to stare into a young girl's eyes and tell her that, even if he had fathered her, he had no interest in her, and never would.

'Mike, your result is here too, and guess what Mike? You *. . . are not the father!'*

Mike jumped up, punched the air, and starting shouting words that would be keeping the people with the swear word bleep busy. Then he gave Jim a high five, and sat back down, legs apart, arrogant in triumph. These over-grown adolescents were acting as though someone had just scored a goal, rather than realising a young girl's search for a father was coming to a dead end, even if her motives weren't the best.

Mike started into a another tirade at Hayley, but Ross didn't want to be short-circuited and miss the opportunity to go for Hayley's jugular himself.

'What a turn up for the books, eh, Hayley? How about it, none of these men are your biological father! Maybe that's for the best, if all you're interested in is money for drink and drugs. Maybe it would be better all round if you never track your real dad down. Perhaps you'd like to apologise to each of these three men you dragged here with your unfounded accusations.'

Hayley looked devastated. The audience cheered and clapped, the men were beaming. Ross was glaring at Hayley like she was something he'd found on the sole of his shoe, and it was then I lost it.

I screamed across the studio. Every head turned my way – the 'fathers', Ross, the camera crew, the audience – it was like they were turning in unison to watch a serve at

Wimbledon. But there was nothing graceful about my delivery, just a volley of words.

'How dare you! How dare you exploit a young girl like that! You're so high and mighty, with your sanctimonious little lectures – well here's one for you – you're the biggest loser in the building, Mr Daley, and looking at what's on the stage here' – I pointed at Mike – 'that's really saying something!'

'Hayley, please come with me – now!'

She didn't resist. Shouldering producers aside, I stormed out of the studio and shoved Hayley into my car. They followed us and even tried to stick a camera in my face, but I blocked it with a well aimed elbow. We whisked off, as though we were under attack in a war zone, which, in a way, we were.

I looked over at her. Her cheeks were moist from tears, but it was like she was refusing to have a good full-on cry. On the way home she was subdued and quiet. Just before she got out of the car, she spoke up.

'Thanks for being with me. I guess I'm like you now, eh? I don't have a dad either. Whoever he is, he might as well be dead like yours. I'm sorry your dad died. It's so sad. Thanks for being with me today.'

I didn't know what to say, so I nodded. Then she gave me a half smile, got out of the car, lit up a cigarette and sauntered into her house.

Later

Went out for a curry with Dex tonight.

He asked me to tell him more about my dad, said he wished that he could have met him. I talked almost non-stop, and he listened and looked interested.

We talked about the Daley debacle. Then he said something that might just mean that I am in love with him.

'He'd be so proud of you today, Helen. You stood up for what matters. Your dad did that with crooked councilors and the powers that be, and he managed to get a youth club for Frenton. You're your father's daughter. You would've made him proud.'

Wow. Wondered if kissing would still be a good idea after a shared Chicken Madras. It was a very good idea indeed.

TUESDAY, JUNE 22nd

Lunchtime

Visited Hayley today to see if she was alright after yesterday's debacle. Weird. It's like it never happened. She said she didn't want to talk about it and that was that. Her unwillingness to talk meant Mrs Tennant shared her theories with me that all priests are paedophiles, it's proven, she said. I made my excuses and fled. At least Hayley doesn't seem to be too damaged by the whole experience, although who knows – she's probably covering up what she really feels anyway.

After work I went to pick up a few bits in the High Street and bumped into Kristian who, strangely, was sitting on the pavement. For a moment I wasn't sure it was him. He was dressed in an old pair of suit trousers and a dirty ripped T-shirt, sitting next to a well-known local homeless man called Ron. Ron is notorious for muttering on about government conspiracies, and drawing diagrams in chalk on the street about which secret organisations are in cahoots with each other. He would probably find it challenging to be in cahoots with anybody, as he's also very smelly. Kristian was holding a plastic cup in front of him and asking people for change.

'Kristian' I hissed, 'What are you doing? You can't ask people for their money, I happen to know you live in a swanky flat in the good part of town!'

'I'm empathising', he replied, 'Becoming one of the poor so I can better connect with them, and pray for them. This is my new friend, Ron, meet Helen.'

He put his arm around Ron's shoulders, and then sniffed the air and removed it.

'Ron's been telling me about how the Catholic church rules the world in cahoots with the Rothschilds and the Gettys. He's got some interesting theories.'

I left him to it. He can bother the homeless folk and leave us women alone. Unless he ends up bothering homeless women . . .

Later

My world has imploded.

Had a quick drink with Dex tonight before he started his shift. We talked a bit more about the *Ross Daley Show*, and then he told me he's thinking of moving out of his aunt and uncle's place. He says they're lovely but he's worried he might wear out his welcome – he only planned to be with them for a week or two when he first arrived. They do have their tendency, as Christians, towards little rules and regulations. He says they don't inflict their principles on him, but he finds himself wanting to debate them endlessly, and that wouldn't be helpful. And they don't like to watch television on Sundays, but Dex likes to catch up on the sport on TV when he's off on on Sunday afternoons, so they tend to go to their bedroom and read, which is awkward.

And then a horrid thought struck me, and there were explosions in my skull. I know exactly who the spy is, leaking the details of our selection committee. I can't believe I haven't seen it before.

The spy – well, informant – is *me*, even though I haven't known it. I am the unwitting quisling. I'd jabbered on to Dex about what was going on, which candidates we were meeting, what our decisions were, and he, probably innocently, had told his aunt and uncle. And their names were Hemming.

I couldn't breathe. The happy-go-lucky hippies who had been damaged by controlling churches: Mr and Mrs Hemming. Dex is their nephew!

I don't know if Dex noticed the blood had drained from my face. He was still talking animatedly about Sunday football, but for the first time since I've met him, I had absolutely no capacity to listen. I felt sick. I grabbed my phone and looked at it, to give an impression I'd got an urgent social worker message. 'I'm sorry, I've got to go, Dex, right now. I'll talk to you soon.'

And I fled. He called after me, but I shouted back over my shoulder that I'd catch him later, trying to play down my sudden exit. He didn't follow me, probably because it was time for his shift to start.

I can't believe it. Dex is related to the Hemming.

Went home via a long walk along the Prom to try to sort out my head. Dex texted *Are you okay?* and I've responded, *I'm fine, will explain later. Sorry I had to rush off like that.*

Okay. Even though this is terribly premature, the possibility of marrying into the Hemmings family fills me with dread, even being distantly related to them. There'd be family reunions when I'd have to see them. I would have to be nice to them, on a regular basis. Word would get out that I was part of the same family, and I could end up being associated with their carping.

I'm probably over reacting, but I can't take any surprises right now: my appetite for the unexpected disappeared when Dad died. I want my life to be uncomplicated and secure. Whenever I get an message at work that's urgent, or Brian calls with news of yet another Hemming missile, my heart starts beating nineteen to the dozen and I can feel myself getting breathless. Not sure if that's what a panic attack is, but I hate the sickly feeling in my stomach and the sense of being overwhelmed. Perhaps this stuff with Dex and the Hemmings doesn't matter much – or perhaps it matters terribly. Am very confused.

WDNESDAY, JUNE 23rd

Restless night last night. Had a dream that included Mrs Hemming dressed as a bridesmaid – my bridesmaid! She had that supercilious sneer on her face as she followed me down the aisle, and looked like a gigantic meringue.

Woke up this morning trying to get my head around the news that Dex had been feeding information to the Hemmings. So that's why the mysterious 'watch-woman' seemed to know so much about what was going on in NWCF, because I was telling Dex and he was telling his aunt and uncle. Me, the wicked wench who had been spotted fleeing from Aaron's flat early in the morning! I'd have thought they wouldn't have wanted their nephew hanging out with an allegedly wanton type like me. But knowing Mrs Hemming's twisted thinking, she probably saw our getting together as the means by which 'the Lord' revealed what was going on at NWCF to her, so she kept quiet. If she finds out I have rumbled her, she will probably tell Dex about me running out of Aaron's flat early that morning. After all, she wrote to the church committee about it. She is sure to tell Dex in her own good time. And what will he think of me, if he knows?

All very bewildering. I think about Dex's open and trustworthy face; he probably didn't think he was doing anything wrong, it's not like I insisted he couldn't tell anyone about the machinations of NWCF. I'm sure the Hemmings have bombarded him with questions, which he most likely felt obliged to answer, seeing as he was living as a guest in their home.

Text arrived from Dex: *Desperate to see you, but boss has called and I have to work a double shift today. Let's get together soon.*

After an uneventful work day (found it difficult to concentrate) I held an emergency meeting at Marinabean with Laura and V.

Laura felt I was being hasty. 'Don't you think you might be panicking a bit? It's not the end of the world. He probably didn't think there was any harm in talking about what's been happening at NWCF to his aunt and uncle. Don't forget, he's not had the history with them you have.'

But that doesn't work for me, and that's part of my problem. I think a three year old would only have to be around the Hemmings for two minutes to pick up they're critical snipers who love to tear others down. I said so, and V jumped in:

'But maybe Dex was trying to believe the best about them. You've told us he doesn't like to be cynical or rush to be critical of others. Maybe he was trying to be generous to them. Don't forget, he knows about their background and how they've been hurt, they were idealistic hippies gone wrong. Sometimes when you know people's stories, and you understand their struggles, you're more forgiving towards them.'

I'd like all this to be true, and perhaps it is, but I'm appalled – maybe irrationally – that Dex has got anything to do with the Hemmings. I don't think it's a deal breaker – I don't want it to be – but Dex and I need to talk all this through. Perhaps my problem is disappointment. After the turbulence of Aaron, it's been wonderful to have a 'normal' boyfriend, and now there are these complications. And I feel stupid about blabbing the details of our committee as well, because it means it's *my* fault we've been getting these spiteful letters from Mrs Hemming.

I said so, and then V piped up: 'You don't know for certain Dex has been saying anything to his aunt and uncle about what we've been going through at NWCF. They might be getting their information from somewhere else. Sit down and talk to him – get some clarity.'

I'd like to talk to Dex about his relatives, but I don't want to get into accusing or even confronting him. What if V is right and it turns out they were getting the information about our church stuff from somewhere else? Unlikely as that seems, I don't want to ruin what is the best thing that has happened to me for ages – and all because of speculation. Am still trying to get my head around still liking him yet knowing who his relatives are, and while I admit it's confusing (keep worrying Mrs Hemming's face is going to pop into my head next time we kiss – if there is a next time), I think I can get over that.

Things between me and Dex have been going so well, that I regularly pinch myself to check I'm not dreaming. Not only is he a throughly nice guy, with no weirdness, he also has the physique of an Adonis on steroids. And he's a Christian but so sensible with it. But he's a Christian from the pedigree stock of Hemming. Rats.

Later

All in all, a terrible day. I know we are going to have to get together soon. Not sure if I can stand waiting – or can stand getting together. Am freaked out. Late tonight got another text from Dex: *Have taken tomorrow off work. Can I cook you dinner tomorrow? We can talk. Dx.*

Yikes. Looks like we're going to finally thrash this thing out.

It has occurred to me this dinner suggestion is perfect. Assuming he doesn't want to cook me dinner at *my* place, then the only location for this gastronomic event will be his place – i.e., the Hemmings' place. Perhaps they'll be there (painful) but then later I'll be able to talk with him about everything without ever having to be confrontational (slightly less painful than it might have been). I can casually ask if he's ever talked to his aunt about the things I've told him.

Perfect. Well, not perfect. Perfect would be no Hemming involvement in my love life, but that would be asking too much. Must try and be chilled out about all of this.

THURSDAY, JUNE 24th

I am so angry.

And after my hope to be a more chilled out person, I am now a human microwave. Here's what happened. Dex texted this morning and said he'd cook dinner at his place, so I set off to the place I've nicknamed in my mind as Hemming Towers. I've never been to Chez Hemmings before. When they were in the church we weren't that close, to say the least. Thought it would be interesting to see their lair. I mean home.

I decided if amateur sleuthing was good enough for Aaron, then I could change my name to Sherlock too. Had decided it was most likely that his aunt and uncle wouldn't be around – after all, Dex said he'd planned lunch and wanted to talk, and that would hardly be possible with them there, would it? But then I thought I could have a little snoop around, and perhaps come upon a photograph of them, which would enable me to naturally raise them in a 'Oh, so *these* are your relatives, are they?' kind of nonchalant way.

Anyway, the house was not at all what I would have expected from the Hemmings. I was expecting a typical 1950s affair, with chintzy sofas and even three ducks flying across some particularly foul paisley wallpaper. The house was not quite ultra-trendy, but certainly modern, with a cool kitchen (dark laminates with lots of chrome and some rather fabulous granite, black with silver grain). And a plush leather three-piece suite in their sitting-room, with a charcoal Berber carpet.

When I arrived he was dashing around in the fab kitchen. He smiled that glorious smile and said 'So glad to see you, Helen. I know we need to talk . . . something seemed to upset you the other night, and I want to know what it is – and if it's anything to do with me, something I said or did, I'm sorry. But let me get lunch sorted, and then we can eat and talk.'

He was making a seafood risotto, with spinach salad and he had a lovely New Zealand white wine (a Marlborough, my favourite) chilling in the fridge. While he was cooking, I popped off to the loo, and on the way back had a quick snoop around the sitting-room. I was disappointed. There were a few baby pictures, but nothing of the Hemmings. No matter, I'd tell him what had upset me.

But then we sat down for the meal. The risotto was delicious, and the wine perfect, tangy and melony but not sharp. This was so lovely. I felt as if I didn't want to ruin this wonderful moment with my anxieties. Just sitting across from Dex, my worries about his relatives seemed irrelevant. Why didn't I forget the whole thing, and tell him I'd had a panic attack and needed to get some air? No, he wouldn't buy that, and besides, I'd be giving him the impression I was an unpredictable saddo who might wreck an evening on a whim by fleeing into the night. I so hated ruining everything by getting into the Hemming issue, but they were the proverbial elephant in the room.

'Dex, this is a fantastic meal, thanks so much. I appreciate it.'

Dex flashed that lovely smile that made me want to abandon the Hemming conversation in favour of some kissing, but I needed to sort this out, and besides, we were still eating.

'No problem. Awesome to have you here. I've been worried since the other night . . . I know you texted to say everything was okay, and I've been telling myself you had some kind of work emergency come up, but I've not been able to put my mind at rest. Are we okay?'

I smiled. 'Of course we are – but there's something I need to get sorted. You know the stuff I told you about NWCF, and all our leadership committee gossip . . . I need to know – did you tell your aunt and uncle about it?'

Dex's brow furrowed, and he looked down at his food for a second or two. 'I did, Helen, and I told them about me and you. We nattered on about you being a social worker, I mentioned your television appearance on the *Ross Daley Show*, and then they asked the inevitable question about whether you were a Christian or not. I wanted to let them know you were right at the heart of NWCF, even on the leadership selection committee. I suppose I wanted them to know you're a Christian who's respected in your church. The conversation went on from there. I didn't tell them much, just mentioned the various candidates you guys have been interviewing. It was more to make conversation than anything. Have I dropped you in it? Have I done something wrong?'

I put my hand on his arm. He looked even more adorable with that worried look in his eye and perfectly furrowed brow. 'It's not you've done anything wrong – it's just you told me yourself your aunt and uncle tend to be legalistic, because of their own struggles when they first became Christians. I would have thought you'd know telling them wasn't the best idea . . . they might use the information you've passed on to them to hurt people.'

Now Dex looked worried. 'Hurt people? My aunt and uncle might be a bit intense, but one thing I know for sure – they wouldn't hurt a soul.'

My heart sank. My surfer god may be great on the waves, but he was useless when it came to discerning people's character. Anyone who had ever been within fifty yards of the Hemmings would know their capacity to be toxic.

'Dex, I know you try to believe the best of people, but surely you can see what I'm worried about. Your aunt has been using the information you gave her to send hurtful anonymous letters to Brian, the chairman of our committee. Each time we've met a new candidate, I've told you, you've told them, and hey presto, we get another poisonous pen-letter in the mail. And to top it all, one of those letters was a very pointed attack on me.'

Dex shook his head in disbelief. 'Sorry, but my aunt and uncle are among the kindest people I've ever met.'

I nearly choked on my risotto. Mrs Hemming kind? I would never have contemplated the words *Hemming* and *kind* appearing in the same sentence.

'For your information, my mother slapped your aunt's face at Dad's funeral because she was so thoughtless and unpleasant, and I was delighted to be there to see it.'

'Helen, I don't think so. I mentioned the tragedy of your dad's death to my aunt, and she said she'd never met him but she'd heard he was a good man, and there had been a huge turnout for his memorial service in the town. But I didn't know they attended it.'

Now I was getting steamed up. 'Maybe that's because they were embarrassed by their rude and disruptive behaviour there. I can't believe you're defending them. They are vicious.'

At which point Dex got flustered. 'Sorry, I'm not going to have you talk about my relatives like that. They're good-hearted people.'

That's when I lost it. My temper rarely flares. but when it does, it really erupts. 'Good-hearted people? You can't be serious! Your aunt is a calculating, cold-hearted, vicious cow, and if you can't see that, then you must be blind! Perhaps you should ask your precious aunt to fill you in on her letter writing hobby. And maybe you should open your eyes. Your aunt with a so-called good heart has a viper of a tongue. I'm one of many who have been bitten. Believing the best is one thing. But being oblivious to what's as obvious as the nose on your face – that's stupid.'

And I made my second hasty exit from a New Zealander's company in a week. I'm not sure whether it was because I didn't want to make things worse, or because I was embarrassed about the 'obvious as the nose on your face' jibe (which was unintended) – or perhaps I didn't want him to see me cry. But I grabbed my coat and bag, marched out and slammed the door behind me. As I escaped, Dex didn't say another word. Nor did he come after me.

I'm back at my flat endlessly rerunning the conversation and battling with being aghast at Dex's unwillingness to face the obvious facts about his aunt from hell, but wondering too whether I've overreacted. When I exploded, I found myself almost watching myself melt down – it was like I was listening to my own voice and realising I was going off the deep end but apparently had no ability to shut myself up. Weird.

Called V, and am confused (or maybe uncomfortable by being confronted) by her comments. 'Dex is showing one of the most important character traits. Loyalty. His aunt and uncle have been good to him, and they probably put on a good show for him too. He's not known you very long, so it's natural he'd come down on their side.'

I explained Mrs Hemming would be completely unable to hide her consistently acidic personality, and while loyalty was important, discernment and wisdom were vital too. 'True, but self control is on the list too – and from the sounds of it, what with your jab about his nose and calling his aunt a cow, you didn't get ten out of ten in that department.'

Had to admit she was right about that. Calling Mrs Hemming a cow was over the top. And I'm cringing as I think about the nose comment, knowing how sensitive Dex is about his adorable hooter. That's the trouble with words. They shoot out of our mouths like athletes from the starting blocks. Well, out of my mouth anyway.

Have looked at my phone fifty times to see if Dex called and left a message while I was talking to V. No call. No message. No text. No Dex.

No more energy. Need sleep.

Woke up feeling fine, and then I remembered yesterday's debacle, and felt sick in my stomach. Lord knows I'm desperate to patch things up with Dex, but I don't know how. I can say sorry for my little nuclear reaction, but the real problem is I can't change my mind about Mrs Hemming. She is what she is, and I can't pretend otherwise. And Dex is in the same dilemma – he can't very well change his mind about her, either, if he doesn't see her bad side, and I don't want to be the one to further enlighten him. So what to do?

Uneventful day at work, Maeve even greyer than usual, if that's possible. Sometimes I think that woman is a character out of an old black and white movie. After her ten minute droning monologue this morning about mileage claims for home visits, I'd wish she'd been in black and white *silent* movies.

At lunchtime I ended up sitting in the seafront cafe trying to think about the situation between me and Dex. I still like him, and I know I'm sounding like a broken record, but I can't believe all this Hemming business. Maybe he has got one of those dormant genes that kicks in the minute he hits 35, turning him into a carbon copy of Mr Hemming. Maybe it's catching and we'll patch things up and get married and then I'll turn into Mrs Hemming and have to buy a horrible little dog and then I'll end up with a face like hers.

I was parked in the exact cafe that Aaron took me to on one of our first dates, where we listened to poetry, had too much red wine and ended up swinging around lamp-posts making up silly songs. I remembered when Aaron used to be so much fun . . .

And then Aaron walked in. At first I thought he hadn't noticed me. In fact he seemed preoccupied with the two girls he brought along. They looked young. They looked thin. They looked much more interesting than me. Dressed in high waisted jeans and vintage lace tops, they were laughing at everything he said. I didn't realise he could be so funny. He looked better though. His hair was washed and his body language seemed more free, less defensive. And he was smiling. Really smiling. Not ironically, or shyly: just genuinely smiling.

Ended up hanging around for the rest of my lunch hour with Aaron. Feel slightly guilty. I suppose I am still officially Dex's girlfriend – at least, we've haven't formally ended things, just had a epic row that hasn't been sorted yet. And it's not like anything happened between me and Aaron. It was strictly a friendship thing. Whilst attempting to sneakily leave the cafe, I managed to trip over a chair, knock over two wineglasses and generally make a spectacle of myself. Of course he noticed and came over to pick me up. The two too-cool-for-school girls shot me curious looks and nudged each other, giggling, probably wondering if I was some sort of social project. He asked if I was leaving, I said yes, he said him too, and we left – without another word to those girls.

We had a heart to heart on the beach. He apologised again for upsetting me with his 'project' and confessed he didn't realise how much his obsession with finding my father's murderer had taken over his life. It wasn't until I had seen the board that he truly understood it was strange. I said we should forget it now and asked him about the giggly girls.

'I've started going to a poetry night – it happens upstairs in the Crown and Anchor pub – I met them there, and they asked if I wanted coffee, which I sadly agreed to.' He made a little face. 'Couldn't shake them off. I think they thought I was some sort of famous poet.'

He said he was glad I had met Dex – and I think he meant it.

'So why the weird staring routine when you saw us on the beach together, Aaron? It was a bit sinister.'

'Sorry. When I saw him and it was obvious you were together, I had this overwhelming anxiety, and felt I wanted to protect you from anyone that might hurt you. You've had so much hurt in your life what with your dad dying, and I suppose I was checking him out and wondering if he's a good bloke. Sorry if it looked odd. I seem to be good at making what is normal look odd.'

I decided not to tell Aaron about Dex being a member of the Hemming family, or the fact our relationship is currently suspended. Aaron said he thought I deserved someone great. Mmm.

And that was it. I said I had to get to get back to work, so we said goodbye with a sort of sideways hug that even Kristian would be proud of. So why do I feel guilty? I feel like I've betrayed Dex in some way, even though I've done nothing wrong. Life is *very* complicated. At least my life is.

Just received a text message from Dex. *Sorry. Can we talk soon? Working tonight. Dx.* Don't know how to respond. Church meeting to vote on John tonight. Oh dear. I texted Dex back, *I'm sorry too. When? Hx.*

No response – but then Friday nights are mad at Fish Sticks.

Off to church for the meeting.

Later

A dreadful end to a dreadful week. I thought Brian was wise to allow things to calm down after John the mighty man of faith and power 'tried out' last week. It would have been wrong to make a decision in the wake of an evening that stirred so many emotions. But now I think the decision to delay the vote until tonight has backfired. It seems like a bomb has gone off in the church. I spent a few minutes before the meeting chatting with him about what's been happening. His healing is 'holding' by the way. Not sure whether to be glad or sad about that.

Anyway, he said that, as a member of the committee, I should know what's going on. He's had a string of emails from one family who are obviously ganging up together – there are a few of them in the church, and they've been involved with NWCF for a thousand years between them (slight exaggeration perhaps) so they seem to think they have the right to control what's happening. They loved John, and are upset because Brian didn't go ahead and vote last Sunday, 'when the anointing was in the house.' When Brian explained he'd felt it was better to wait and pray, they said we had missed the anointed moment. Am bewildered by this logic. Why would God get in a huff with us for waiting and praying before making an important decision? Even as I said this to Brian, felt very guilty because I don't think I have prayed a single prayer about John or the vote. Been too busy pondering Dex, now probably my ex-boyfriend.

Then Brian said one of the family 'gang' emailed back to say they feel they 'haven't been heard.' Brian said he'd wanted to write back and say they have been heard, but they're still wrong. Brian said 'being heard' is not the same as being agreed with. It means we're given a fair hearing. This family have said they are not going to give any more money to the church until this is properly resolved – which, I think, means resolved their way. Sounds like blackmail to me.

Why can't we disagree more agreeably? We're going to have conflicts, I know that, and I'm glad – I want to be in a healthy church, not a cult.

Brian said he'd had 34 emails in all, some of them saying John is the key to our church's future, others saying if he ever steps foot in our church again, they'll leave. And there have been a couple of spiteful ones accusing the selection committee of being irresponsible for even allowing John to try out. Then Brian had a phone call from an angry person who yelled at him and said he was trying to sabotage the possibility of John being appointed, by delaying the vote. Poor old Brian. He's experiencing that joyous feeling that comes when you know whatever you do, you'll upset someone. I wish the church could see our hearts and motives. We've been meeting for long hours, unpaid, we didn't ask for the job, and all we get is grief. Even the Alpha course is in a state. Laura said at work yesterday that during the 'Any questions' slot at the end of the evening, someone asked why is being pushed over part of praying for healing – and then the whole thing descended into a row. Hayley had showed up again, and announced loudly that if some preacher tried to push her around, she'd kick him hard where it hurts. Not helpful.

And if all that's not enough, Alan, the poor man who lost his wife and then child last year has formally tendered his resignation from the church. Brian got an email from him yesterday afternoon – he says he can't be in a church where illness and grief are not acknowledged, and he was made to feel the terrible losses in his family were his fault because he didn't have enough faith or authority. He described the evening with John as sheer torture. For others, it was heavenly. I don't get how John could create such a total love/hate reaction. I'm hoping this problem gets sorted, fast. I wish Robert and Nola were here. The plastic sheep are getting scattered. Speaking of V's plastic sheep, I've been wondering how she would behave tonight. I soon found out.

Brian and I finished our chat and we dragged ourselves into the meeting with heavy hearts, fearing the worst, which was probably prophetic. There was a big turn-out – perhaps the promise of a blood-letting is a draw.

Brian called for order, which didn't immediately settle everyone down. The best way to shut Christians up is announce a prayer, which he did, and then asked God for wisdom, grace and direction in our discussions. Not sure how much of that prayer was answered.

'I'd like to open the floor now for discussion: let's try to stay focussed on the issue – should John be invited to be the new leader of NWCF?'

V immediately jumped up. 'I've been grateful to be a member of the selection committee, and I have to say, as far as I'm concerned, there isn't anything to discuss, and so . . .'

Brian interrupted.

'Vanessa, I know that you hold strong opinions, but I do feel it right to say that your membership of that committee means that you have had plenty of opportunity to express them. It's only fair that others who are not committee members should be given the chance to speak.'

V wasn't dissuaded. She looked right at him: 'This is simple. Did you get healed or not? If there's one thing we need in our church, it's more of the power of God at work. And when John came, we saw some of that raw power unleashed. What greater confirmation do we need? He's our man. That is all I have to say.'

It was pandemonium. There were some who thought V was absolutely right, and we should get on with it and take the vote without any further delay. Then someone said we didn't need a leader who pushed people around when they prayed. Then Kristian got up and spoke in those long ponderous tones that people sometimes use when they think they're saying something deep.

'I liked John, although I did think that he tried to impinge upon my anointing as a worship leader.'

I marvelled. 'Impinge upon my anointing?' Sometimes Christians come up with the most ridiculous phrases.

Kristian continued, even slower now.

'I could never lead worship in a church where this prosperity message is taught. It is just so dishonouring to the poor. This means a lot to me; in recent months I've been receiving more and more songs from God about the poor, and I feel that God is speaking through me as a prophetic minstrel to NWCF, and perhaps, who knows, beyond?'

Gag. Once again Kristian was making it all about him.

From there it went from bad to worse. Voices got louder, and there was even some fist-shaking going on. Someone suggested we were being racist – the real problem was that John was a black man, and our nervousness had nothing to do with his theology, it was his ethnicity that troubled us.

Brian tried to call for order, and as he was trying to say that we should calm down and treat each other with more respect, someone – I'm not sure who it was because of a lot of people were trying to talk over him – shouted 'Shut up!' I thought he was going to crumple. A look of utter defeat spread across his face, as if someone had punched him. I knew there was a good chance that he would simply walk out of that meeting and never come back. And I also realised that I had seen something like this very recently, during the *Ross Daley Show*, when people were treated with cruelty. That's exactly what we were doing – but this was church, we were the people who were supposed to be followers of Jesus, and we were behaving in a way that was no different from the audience on the Daley show.

I still can't believe I did it. I walked to the microphone, snatched it off the stand with attitude, and looked at Brian and said, 'Don't move.' Okay, it was a bit *CSI*, but at least I didn't tell him to freeze.

And then I let loose. I can't remember exactly what I said, but it went something like this:

'I think we need to stop this right now. For the last few months, ever since Robert and Nola left, the atmosphere of our church has been so tense. Brian has worn himself out leading the selection committee – in fact, I'm worried he's making himself ill, he's been under so much pressure. We've spent hours interviewing. We've talked until late in the night. We've endured senseless emails and even had poisonous letters from ex-members of this congregation who have absolutely no business meddling in our affairs. Good friends who've been together for years have fallen out over this; I've even heard that some of us are not talking to each other. Have we forgotten Robert's final sermon to us? "Little children, love one another." And what about all those plastic sheep V told us about? This flock is not only being scattered, it's going to be lamb chops if we carry on like this. And the issue is not whether someone was healed or not. Of course we all want to see more of God's power at work – that isn't in question. But the issue is whether John is the man to lead us into the next chapter as a church. And let's not allow this issue to be clouded over with the race debate. I think we're all above that, even if we are acting like complete idiots right now.

'What do we agree on? We want to be a loving church. We want to be a church that is open to genuine Holy Spirit power. We want to be a church where sound preaching is normal. We want to be a church that Robert and Nola would be proud of. And most of all, we want to be a church that Jesus would be proud of. So why don't we all take responsibility for our attitudes, and if we think we need to, ask God to forgive us?

'And why don't we take the vote, and respect each other's views? Aren't we grown up enough to put aside our differences and believe that somehow, as we vote, God will get his will done? Why don't we vote now?'

And so we did. John didn't get a clear majority, and Brian announced our search would continue. Admittedly, there was some murmuring, but as the meeting ended it did feel like some of the heat had been taken out of the situation. Or maybe not.

Got home tonight and felt sad because Dex has not followed up our texts with a phone call. Okay, logic suggests I could call him, but he is working, and anyway, I'd like him to make the next move, for no reason that makes any sense. Fretted at the silence from my mobile phone until I finally got a message at midnight. *Sorry, mad night here. Coffee tomorrow? Dx.* My stomach is lurching at the thought, but I'm desperate to get things sorted. I like my New Zealander, and I'm hoping somehow we can move through this. Perhaps agree to disagree? Might work in a church conflict, but it's not exactly the best foundation for a close relationship. Texted back: *Marinabean 11am? Hx.*

He responded. *Awesome. Dx.*

Hope it will be awesome. And not awful.

SATURDAY, JUNE 26th

It's a corny old saying, *They said smile, things could be worse, so I smiled, and things did get worse.* Felt out of breath and overwhelmed by the mountain of rubbish happenings in my life right now.

Spent the morning cleaning the flat, and then headed for Marinabean. I was stoked up emotionally. I know this, because I asked for a slice of my favourite carrot cake and almost burst into tears when they said it was all sold out. Got the dull neck ache that comes from tension; what with church and now Dex/Hemmings, I'm wound up like a spring. Then disaster hit. Got there early so I could make an attempt at self-composure; decided I should focus on my over-reaction and apologise to Dex unreservedly for that, and then see how the conversation goes from there. Then, at about 10.50am, he arrived.

Aaron that is. He was stopping by for a chai tea, and then spotted me, smiled broadly and ambled over to the table, and sat down. I went into a flustered meltdown, mumbling about how I was meeting Dex in a few minutes, and he said 'Fine, it would be nice to meet him, say hello and then I'll leave you two in peace.' I panicked and launched into a monologue about the row Dex and I had. Aaron became all protective, said he didn't care if Dex was a surf god, if he was mistreating me, than he'd have him to deal with. I tried to explain things had got out of hand . . .

. . . and then I burst into tears. It was inevitable, I suppose, my heart already having been churned over by the tragic lack of carrot cake. I started blubbering and heads in Marinabean turned around to see what the fuss was all about. Aaron shot around the table, knelt down and put his arms around me. 'Don't cry, Helen, it'll be fine, I will sort him out for you.'

I was trying to say I didn't need anyone to sort anything out, but it came out as an incomprehensible wail. And that's when Dex walked in. I'm wrapped in Aaron's arms whimpering and he stood there, staring at us both. Then he turned around and walked out, without saying a word. Aaron uncurled his arms, and started to go after him, but I shouted at him, which made yet more heads turn. 'Enough! I don't need you to sort this out for me! I'm a big girl!' Aaron mumbled his apologies, and then tried to sit down at the table again. 'I think I need some space, thanks', I said, with enough edge in my voice to ensure he went away pronto.

I immediately phoned Dex, but the call went straight through to the answering machine. Texted *It's not what you think.*

He isn't replying.

Went to Fish Sticks to see if I could find him, but his boss said that he'd called in sick. And I don't dare go around to the Hemmings' lair – the last people I want to witness a row between me and Dex is them.

Texted again. And again. And yet again. Still no reply.

SUNDAY, JUNE 27th

Phoned Dex again this morning, but he's obviously turned his phone off.

Headed for church. There have been some more casualties at NWCF. Brian emailed early this morning to say three more people have already tendered their resignation by email; one left because we didn't vote John in, one resigned because we'd even considered him in the first place, and the third resignation was because of the way we'd all acted at the church meeting.

This morning's service showed a faint glimmer of hope, however. Mr S-B spoke, not an easy task, but his words were so solid and gentle, you could almost sense healing taking place as he prayed at the end. We're not out of the woods yet; conflict doesn't fade away so easily, and the search for the leader continues, which means there's plenty of capacity for a fight to break out again.

Kristian seemed very quiet this morning; he hardly spoke in between songs, which is not his usual style of leading worship. And I noticed that he was quite tearful when he'd finished. Wonder what's happening there . . .

After church I had a natter with Laura, which basically involved me talking non-stop at speed about the Dex situation.

'If you like this guy', said Laura, 'then this is worth fighting for. It looks like a right mess at the moment, but what happened at Marinabean yesterday is easy enough to sort out. And perhaps you can find a way forward with the situation with his relatives. It's complicated, I know, but not insurmountable.'

I think she's right, but I can't see how this can work. Am finding myself in a fixed thinking pattern right now – and it goes like this – life is horrid, has been for a while, I've lost Dad, I've lost Robert and Nola, and now I've lost Dex.

Got back to the flat, and sent yet another text to Dex: *It's a terrible misunderstanding. Let's talk. Please. Hx.*

Finally I plucked up courage and went around to the house, and he was in. Seemed stunned when he opened the door but I think he was pleased to see me, but was so surprised, initially he forgot to ask me in.

'I think we need to talk, Dex. What you saw at the coffee shop the other day was not what it seemed. Can I come in?'

I gingerly stepped over the threshold into the Hemming lair, half expecting the formidable lady would leap out of the shadows, attach herself to my throat, and mercilessly smother me to death in her considerable bosom. Dex sensed my nervousness. 'My aunt and uncle are out shopping, so you're safe – at least for a while.' I laughed too loud which obviously gave away the fact that I was extremely nervous. And so I launched in. 'I'm sorry you walked into the cafe when you did, but it was all perfectly innocent. I was upset because of us, and had a cry, and he was being . . . friendly. Trying to be kind. But there's nothing in it at all.'

'It didn't look too platonic to me. I think you're awesome, but if you want to be with Aaron, that's fine with me. I don't want all this complicated stuff in my life right now. I got myself on an even keel after leaving the discipleship course, and I don't know what to do about your feelings about my relatives. I've racked my brains and have tried to connect your description of them with the people I know, but I can't see my aunt being like that. Maybe blood's thicker than water, and I'm not seeing what they're like, but I'm struggling.'

So that's when I took about five breathless minutes to tell him the complete and relatively unabridged history of Mrs Hemming and me – her anonymous letter writing, her accusing me of being a scarlet woman after the night at Aaron's, everything. He asked me twice if anything had happened with Aaron, but for the most part sat back and listened.

'Wow. This is incredible, I can't believe I've been so oblivious. Maybe I have gone way over the top in my believing the best stuff. If all this is true, I can see why you don't like her. I think I'm going to have to confront my aunt with all this. It's the only way forward.'

And then I heard the key scraping in the door, and the sound of it opening. Mr and Mrs Hemming were back from their shopping trip. This was going to be awkward. I held my breath when they stepped into the kitchen.

Except it wasn't them at all. A slightly older couple, whom I did not recognise, ambled into the room; she tossed her car keys onto the kitchen counter. Did Mr and Mrs Hemming have more relatives staying?

'Hi, Auntie Brenda, Uncle Ron. This is Helen. But I think you guys have already met.'

The lady looked confused, apologised, and said she couldn't remember having met me, but she was very pleased to meet me now. And here I embarrassed myself. Dex was starting to tell his aunt that he knew the whole story about me and her, and they needed to talk, whereupon I said, 'No, you're right, Brenda. We have never met. I am so pleased to meet you. I've heard so many lovely things about you.' I gave them both enormous hugs, the huge relief obviously hijacking my brain cells. They hugged me back, as if such warm embraces were normal between complete strangers.

'But you said . . .' Dex spluttered, and I cut him off before any damage could be done to this new-found beautiful relationship. 'Dex, it's a big misunderstanding. I was mistaken. I'll explain later.' He looked confused.

Anyway, we all had a cup of tea, and he is right. His aunt and uncle are lovely. They seemed nervous when I mentioned a film I'd seen recently (apparently they don't go to the cinema) but didn't comment. At last I managed to say my goodbyes and get Dex out of the house, and we took a long walk along the beach, and I spent most of the time apologising. 'I jumped to conclusions. Your description of your aunt and uncle seemed to fit the Hemmings, and when the anonymous letters started arriving, and I realised you were the only person I'd talked to about our committee stuff, I put two and two together, and came up with five. I'm so terribly sorry. And I shot my mouth off and made comments about your nose that I think is lovely and then it got worse and . . .'

Dex managed to stop me talking, because it's hard to natter when you're kissing. When we finally came up for air, he said jumping to conclusions was easy enough to do, because he'd done the same when he'd walked into Marinabean and seen me with Aaron. Conversation at that point was further inhibited by more kissing.

And then he really shocked me.

'All that stuff I said earlier about it being fine if you decided to be with Aaron? I didn't mean it at all. I just only want you to be with me if that's what you really want. But this mess up between us has made me realise how terrible it would be to lose you. What I'm saying is, I think . . . I'm falling in love with you.' Am not absolutely certain what my precise response was, because it was excited, garbled, and punctuated by quite a lot of kissing. I think I said, 'I think you're wonderful, Dex', which sounds a bit lame. I know I didn't say 'I love you' right out there . . . even though I think I do . . .

Am delirious with joy. Relieved. I don't have to like the Hemmings in order to like (or love?) Dex. Of course, one question remains. Who is the spy who is leaking information to them? One thing's for sure: Mrs Hemming is not related to Dex, and right now, that's all I care about.

MONDAY, JUNE 28th

Woke up this morning with two wonderful thoughts: now things are sorted with Dex, (a) we might end up getting married and gloriously (b) Mrs Hemming won't be a bridesmaid, or even be invited. Hooray and hallelujah.

Laura and V came round to my flat this evening for our monthly prayer triplet, a prayer triplet that has been more of a prayer duo over these last few months. I must admit I have been incredibly slack at attending, and have left it to them. Updated them on my marvellous news concerning missing identities, and love in the air, and they were thrilled.

Anyway, we had a lovely natter and also managed to clear the air after the tension around John the mad prosperity preacher. V was licking her wounds a bit and feels after reflection that she was wrong to jump up in the meeting as she did. Her heart is in the right place, even if sometimes her head is on Jupiter. I do love her. And who am I to criticise others for jumping in?

Spent way too long talking to Dex on the phone after he finished his shift.

THURSDAY, JULY 1st

Am missing Dex, he's been working long hours again. Now we've sorted everything out I want to hang out with him more than ever. Yep, I think it's definitely lurve . . .

Met Brian again for coffee after work.

Had a good talk about how he's doing with all the committee/church meeting dramas. He's been struggling since our church meeting – even though things are better, he's still feeling very bruised. Apparently he found out who it was who yelled 'Shut up' in the meeting, and is feeling angry about being talked to that way. He says he can't bring himself to talk to the person concerned (he won't tell me who it is) and he says he can't forgive them, because they haven't asked for forgiveness. In his typical forensic way, Brian's conclusion is he will forgive when they ask for forgiveness – after all, isn't that the way God works? He waits for us to repent. I said that's true, but the difficulty is that makes us a hostage to the other person's choices. And God didn't wait until we called for help before sending Jesus – he took the huge initiative – while we were yet sinners Christ died for us. He respects our will, and waits to be wanted, but he's already come the extra 10,000 miles towards us. Grace is willing to be bruised in seeking reconciliation. Good old Brian. He is still dull, but he's such a servant, and so willing to listen. Still worried about him though. He doesn't even get excited about debunking Dawkins any more. The light seems to have gone out in his eyes.

I asked what he thought our next step should be in trying to find another leader – and he stunned me with his answer. Brian, who was emphatically against ordinary Sue when she came before, said he'd wondered if we'd made a mistake by not putting her forward to the congregation. He remembered that, despite disagreeing with her on the six day creation stuff, she was 'solid.' Perhaps solid and dependable is what we need. Of course, we don't even know if she is available, but Brian was thinking about phoning V and James to see what they think – as V voted against Sue as well.

Later

Late night email from Brian. V is all for talking to Sue again. James keen too. V said she'd never felt good about the way she had dismissed Sue as being a plodder. God has been dealing with her tendency to let her zeal turn her into making super-swift judgments about people. That's the lovely thing about V. She is deeply spiritual – and knows she can get it wrong. She thought that because the committee had decided not to allow Sue to try out, there was no way back. She is delighted we are approaching Sue again. This is getting interesting.

The other hot news from the church is stunning. Wonders, indeed, will never cease.

Brian said that Kristian had been talking to him over the last few weeks about writing a musical about poverty, and wanting to stage it in the Church Hall. He had already written five of the songs, 'God came to him in a burst of inspiration one afternoon' and apparently he managed to write them all down in an hour and a half.

– 221 –

But that's all changed now. Apparently Kris found the church meeting where he made his big statement about the prosperity gospel hard. He's told Brian that he still believes that, but that he feels God has been showing him that so much of his passion is wrapped up in getting himself and his songs promoted. He's been relooking at some of his 'songs from God' and has decided that they're probably not, because they're not much good. He had a big moment in last Sunday morning's service – that would have been why he was quiet and a bit tearful – and says he wants to make some changes from now on.

Of course, we've seen Kris's reactionary spirituality at work before, with his music video that would change the world, and his solemn vow to avoid the evil that is the female of the species . . . but I'd really like to give him the benefit of the doubt. Perhaps some real change is going on . . .

SATURDAY, JULY 3rd

One of the great mysteries of the Universe has now been solved. At last I know who the spy who leaked our confidential information to Mrs Hemming is. It's Brian. And he is terribly embarrassed about it. It all goes back to when he set up his email loop to communicate with the committee. Apparently he typed each committee member's email address in, and the auto-fill on the computer must have seen the first two letters of my name, 'H-e' and then completed them as 'H-e-mming.' Brian says he made the loop 'blind copy', which means no one else in the loop would have spotted all emails intended for me were in fact being sent to Mrs Hemming instead. Then Brian must have added my name as well. So that's how Mrs Hemming knew so much – without knowing it, Brian was briefing her by mistake, sending her all agendas, minutes – every detail about our process. He is absolutely mortified. He's such a detailed/technical person, and this is not like him at all. I didn't bother to tell him all the grief that had been caused by my trying to be a spy-catcher. He feels bad enough already. But at least the mystery's solved. Phoned Dex tonight and told him, and he giggled. 'Awesome', he said, 'Truly, totally awesome.'

Brian, obviously, has now deleted Mrs Hemming from the email loop, which will stop her supply of information. She'll be livid.

Tonight had some Tex Mex with Dex, how very poetic! We had fajitas and nachos and I have decided Mexican food is my new thing: Mexican food with Dex anyway. This deepening relationship means that I seem to be eating out a lot. Must watch that. Realised I had guacamole on my nose for half the date, which Dex very kindly wiped off for me, tres embarrassing but cute. He's so easy to talk to, and the world seems like a nicer place when he's around. He manages to see the good in everything, and doesn't seem to get stressed out about all the little things in life. I know I shouldn't either but sometimes it's hard to be relaxed when someone barges in front of you in the bus queue or it starts to rain after you've spent half an hour doing your hair, or some hideous television host does his thing. Dex doesn't seem to mind when things go wrong. The waiter brought him the wrong order and Dex, instead of being stressed, seemed to think it was a lovely surprise. Very lovable indeed. Yes.

SUNDAY, July 4th

Church was unexpectedly good. Brian spoke on forgiveness, talked about how we need to forgive whether or not those who have hurt us actually ask for our forgiveness. Said he'd been learning about that in his own life this week, and even quoted me and gave me credit for the quote! I have joined the ranks of C.S. Lewis, etc.

Brian also said we often fail in the areas where we think we are the strongest, which I think was a veiled reference to him being the NWCF mole, while thinking he was a technical genius.

Quick chat after the service with the Kyomos – seems like they are volunteering to become helpers at Alpha. They are definitely getting stuck in at NWCF.

Had a huge Sunday lunch with Mum and then Dex came over to my flat after he finished work: spent the whole evening having a mammoth DVD box-set extravaganza with him. We snuggled on the sofa drinking endless cups of tea. It was exactly what I needed. Feel really close to him now we have navigated our way through our major spat. We've fought in order to stay together.

Endless team meeting today in which I was very nearly miraculously healed of insomnia. I love my job, and the case updates and discussions are helpful, but today I thought Maeve would never stop talking. Fantasised about hitting her at one point. I am glad fantasies are private and not shown on screens above our heads. Am especially glad no on-screen fantasies are on show when I am around Dex.

Sometimes I wonder – if people knew us, would they like us – or even want to have anything to do with us? We're all good at playing the game, but we're all icebergs – only the tip is to be seen, but underneath there's this great mass of . . . well, stuff. Perhaps that's why long term friendships that last a lifetime are rare – the closer we get, the more junk we see, and then we back off, and go looking for another friendly iceberg. Praying I will grow old with the same friends around me. V, James, Laura . . . and Dex.

Brian texted to say he'd placed a call to Sue, which went well. He said he apologised about the way he'd reacted to her before – the events of the last couple of months have taught him that sometimes we get too emphatic and divided, and that, while he still firmly held his views, he respected hers, and wanted to ask if she was willing to come and interview again. He said he'd expected Sue to turn him down flat, but she was very warm and gracious. She understood we'd been on a tough journey and she'd like to come and talk to us again. Brian also talked her through the difficult time we'd had as a church, but she said that, although there would be ongoing challenges, these things were nothing new. Basically human beings behaved the same way over and over – the issues would change, the key players differ, but these squabbles and fights were nothing original, sadly. Anyway, she's coming for a meeting with us this Friday.

Also Brian told me that Kristian has come up with a new concept – and it's radical and not at all what we would have expected from him.

He has totally put all his 'God gave me a song' stuff aside, at least for a moment, and has decided he'd like us to put on an evening about justice – the idea is that the choir will practice six or eight songs about poverty and God's heart for justice, there will be a short film presentation from a charity that are doing an amazing work around the world, called 'Children on the Edge', and then Brian would be asked to give a simple ten minute talk about how we might respond as a church.

But here's the real shocker – none of the songs that we will sing are written by Kristian. He told Brian that he's been sickened as he's pondered his attitudes – so much of what he's done has been self promotion. This will be a wonderful step forward for him, and a real opportunity for the church to look beyond itself and come together to unite on a worthwhile project. Am excited.

Gazillion calories pepperoni (with extra pepperoni) pizza tonight shared with V, James, Laura and Dex. It's the first time Laura, V and James have had the chance to sit down and spend some quality time with Dex and I'm delighted to announce they like him. V thinks beneath the chilled out exterior there's someone who is thoughtful and sincere in their relationship with God. Perhaps she can see a hint of James's solidity in Dex. Laura thought he was lovely too.

I think I've realised what's so great about him. When he meets people, he seems to want to know more about them. His interested silence is not cool and chilled out, it makes people genuinely feel special. It's not rocket science: people pay huge sums of money to go into a room and have the luxury of someone else's undivided attention. I know therapists do more than just listen, but surely being lent an ear (even with a price tag attached to it) is what people crave the most. Have decided to listen more and speak less. Hope this decision will mean some changes in the way I do life.

My mother is relentless now she's heard about Dex. Every time she phones, it's 'And how is Dex?' and 'When do I get to meet him?' and 'Do you think he'll be working in that bar forever?' and 'Does he treat you right? He's not weird like Aaron, is he?'

I think she's expecting to see a ring on my finger any day now. I haven't told Mum yet – but I think that I love him.

WEDNESDAY, JULY 7th

Invited my mother round for dinner at my flat. She was disappointed when I said Dex couldn't come (he's working), but we had a great evening. I made her favourite, fish and salad, after an uber-bout of cleaning shared together. My mother can spot dust from a mile away. We had a lovely girly time, and I realised that as I get older, we are becoming more and more like friends. Of course she will always be my mother, but it is nice having her confide in me like a girlfriend, rather than deciding not to share stuff with me, to protect me. I felt close to her.

Lord, I pray you will help my mum not to feel so lonely. That you will surround her with people who love her and look after her. I pray I can be the best daughter and friend I can be for her.

THURSDAY, JULY 8th

Hayley home visit. Nothing to report, as disinterested grunts aren't worth reporting. Her behaviour at college isn't improving, and they're threatening to remove her from the course if she doesn't shape up soon. Asked her if she wanted to come to church next weekend, and she gave me a flat-out '*No.*' She says she is not interested in Alpha any more either, since the row over John and the threat to kick him and relieve him of the possibility he might father more children. Oh dear.

Also had a planning meeting about Kristian's new idea at NWCF, and I must say, I'm impressed. He listened rather than lectured, and is holding to his idea of a simple evening of song, film, prayer and a short talk – and, again, remarkably, no songs written by him. We're announcing a first rehearsal this weekend.

After the meeting finished, Kris asked to have a word with me. He was nervous.

'There's a couple of things I need to say, and I think they're important. Have you got a minute?'

I was nervous. I'm delighted to see a change in Kris' heart, but whatever next? Was he suddenly going to announce that for ages he's been stifling a deep seated love for me?

'We've never talked about that incident that happened when we were at the conference – you know, me and you, that night we were alone in the chalet and I went to kiss you and . . .'

'Kristian', I said, perhaps a little too firmly, 'there never was a me and you. Out of the blue you just decided that it might be a good idea to get frisky and then . . .'

Kris interrupted. 'I know, you're right. I put that clumsily. I know there was never an us. What I'm trying to say is that I have never apologised for trying it on that night, and I should have. And then when I think of all that you've had to go through with the loss of your dad over the last year or so . . . I should have been the first to ask for forgiveness and at least try to put the mess that I made right. So, I know it's way overdue, but will you forgive me? I've been an idiot. In fact idiot doesn't cut it. Pompous, self obsessed diva more like. Everyone at NWCF has been kind to put up with me . . . and there's something else I want you to know . . .'

I froze. This was very good news so far, which now might be followed up by horrifying news of his undying love for me.

'You triggered me into starting to examine my heart and motives at the church meeting. That speech you made – I'd just got up there and strutted around about downloading songs from God about the poor . . . and then you said we should all examine our hearts, or something like that. I don't know why – maybe it was simply the Holy Spirit at work – but that statement hit me like a ton of bricks. I didn't sleep that night, and for about three days I went on this journey of soul searching that had me in tears most of the time. Anyway, I just wanted to let you know that God used you that night at the meeting. Please forgive me for being such a pain?'

I said that of course he was forgiven (and I know I meant it), and gave him a big hug, which he didn't feel the need to resist.

Caught up with Dex at the end of his shift, and told him about Kris. He seemed pleased. Then he told me about some of the scrapes he got into growing up in New Zealand (which I think would be a nice place to honeymoon). Yikes. Did I say honeymoon?

FRIDAY, JULY 9th

Interview with 'solid' Sue tonight. She is lovely. She was so gracious about the tense meeting we had before, and Brian seemed to make a special effort to make her feel at home. She said that, if we would like to invite her, she's very willing to come and preach. However, she has stipulated she will only accept an invitation to be our minister if there is an 80% vote in her favour (rather than a majority) because she needs a clear mandate to take the church through the challenging process of healing after our recent traumas. We unanimously agreed we'd like her to preach for us, which she's going to do the weekend after next.

SATURDAY, JULY 10th

Spent the whole day with Dex. Beautiful sunny day, so I made sandwiches, and we picnicked. Had another one of those conversations about God's will – only this time it got *really* interesting. We munched our sandwiches, and then sat there, nattering about nothing much for a while. Dex was casually lobbing pebbles into the sea.

'Can I ask a question about relationships?'

For a moment, I felt a slight hint of panic, wondering if Dex still had any lingering concerns about Aaron. But I needn't have worried.

'Do you think that there's such a thing as "The One"? You know, the one person we should marry? I've heard that idea taught quite a lot – they were big on it at the discipleship school – don't make a move towards deepening any relationship until you're absolutely sure that you've found "The One", God's perfect and only choice for you as a partner. In fact some people took it so far, they wouldn't date, saying that they'd prefer to pray, and when God revealed the name of "The One" to them, then they'd develop a friendship, and then marriage. But I don't buy it. What do you think?'

So I told him exactly what I thought. I don't buy this idea at all. For one thing, I've seen people get totally tied up in paranoia because of this – they fall in love, but are then terror struck that perhaps the one they love is not "The One" – and go through emotional agony as a result. I've also known of one or two Christians who got married 'because the Lord told us to', but missed out on the rather important detail of loving the person, with predictably disastrous results.

'Yeah, I've seen a bit of that too. I suppose the other important thing is, even though people teach this stuff, the Bible doesn't say that there is only one person who is right for you. When you think about it, that can't be true. What about if you get married, and your partner dies, and you marry someone else? Does that mean God has a special "Number Two" person held in reserve? Or what if you went through a divorce, and then remarried – is that new person the new "One"? I think we make all this stuff more complicated than it needs to be.'

So I asked him how he planned to make big decisions for the future.

'Having started the discipleship school, and then leaving – with all that going wrong, I suppose I think that God's purposes for me are not narrow and fixed. I don't think that I'm doing his will just because I've had some big guidance. God knows, and I've thought a lot about this, that I want what he wants. So I'm going to just keep on making myself available. I want to pray about my decisions, ask for wisdom, and build friendships where other people can help me too. But I don't want to get myself freaked out about the whole thing.'

And that seems to me to be a very good answer.

Dex had planned to surf for a while this afternoon, and I had planned to watch him (!), but the wind dropped and the sea, for once, was too flat. He had to be at work at 4pm, so I headed back to the flat. Relaxing evening watching television, punctuated only by a text from him. *Thanks for a great day. Loads of love. Dx.*

SUNDAY, JULY 11th

Brian announced in church this morning that next weekend Sue is coming to preach as a potential ministerial candidate. And Kris announced the musical evening. First practice this week.

Met Dex after church and we had a cheeseburger on the Prom. Dating definitely makes you put on weight and I have been gaining pounds steadily with all the food we end up eating! After, he came back to mine for coffee, and that's how he got to meet my mother – at last. It wasn't on purpose, and normally your mother meeting your new boyfriend would be more of an official and scary affair, but there's something so chilled out about Dex that he manages to find situations which would normally reduce me to a trembling wreck bearable, even positively enjoyable. We were sipping coffee when my mother phoned. She's bought a new cabinet for the sitting-room but the delivery men had left it in the hall and she couldn't lift it all by herself. Dex overheard the conversation and piped up he wouldn't mind helping her out and this very afternoon would be perfect, as we had yet to make any plans.

I initially hesitated, but then I thought . . . why not? It was unlikely I would be much help hauling furniture, and this would give my mother, who has been dying to meet Dex, the perfect opportunity. I told Mum we would be there soon so we jumped in the car and drove over to her place.

Mum greeted Dex with a huge hug that made the Prodigal Son's homecoming look like a cold shoulder, and thanked him at least thirty times for coming to her aid with the furniture. The natter over a cup of tea went well, although there were moments when it seemed Mum was asking a few too many questions, but I'm probably being over-sensitive. Then Dex got down to the job in hand. Whilst he heaved the cabinet into the sitting-room my mother bustled round in the kitchen, managing to whip up an Italian feast in a matter of minutes, and stuck it on the kitchen table, so we didn't have much choice when she asked us if we would be staying for supper. Dex was positively ravenous, I think that man could eat an entire cow in one sitting. My mother started asking him yet more questions about his plans. Did he think he'd stay in England? Was he going to be working at Fish Sticks forever? Was he planning on moving into his own place at some point . . .?

Dex said he has fallen in love with England, and he was hoping to stay here indefinitely. He told Mum that long term he wants to set up his own surf school and, as part of it, teach kids who are vulnerable how to ride the waves – a sort of surf therapy. He mentioned that during his teenage years he had struggled, and surfing had given him something to do and helped him sort out his issues. He said the adrenalin it gave you made you feel amazing, and it gives you time to think about your life and what you are doing. Every time I learn more about him, I am pleasantly surprised. There's such a lot going on beneath his chilled out vibe. As we left my mother gave me a wink and whispered quietly to me he was a keeper. I'm thinking she's definitely right . . .

Bummer. Have discovered I must have left my purse in the cheeseburger joint. Phoned them immediately but they can't find it, which means some nasty piece of work must have picked it up and made it their own.

Now have to phone my credit card company (okay, companies, I have three) to cancel my cards. Boring.

MONDAY, JULY 12th

Wonders will never cease. At lunchtime today I popped into the police station to see if my purse had been handed in – and it was! Some lovely person must have felt nervous about handing it in at the burger place so was kind enough to trek to the police station and hand it over. Delighted. I wasted about an hour last night cancelling my credit cards, but this is a better result. Also will have to wait until the new ones come through before I can spend any money, as these are now useless.

TUESDAY, JULY 13th

Hayley is so unpredictable. Went to see her today, and she was weird. Seemed distant and spaced out, but yet wanting to talk about the situation with her 'dad' who never was her dad. And even though she was engaging in conversation, it was all disjointed, confused. Wondered if she was on something today. I wanted to ask her if she'd decided not to come to church or Alpha any more, but had Maeve's words of warning about pressurising her running through my mind, so I left it.

Then Hayley started talking about my dad, which was strange. 'You had something cool, there, in your dad, Helen. I think good dads are rare. Seems like such a waste he lost his life like he did. And all because he tried to protect someone who was being mugged. A life for a wallet with a few quid in it. Such a waste.'

Am worried about Hayley – she was in a state, and when I got up to leave, she started to cry. I went over to comfort her, and she said there was something she was trying to sort out, she'd be fine. And then, out of the blue, she came running out after me and gave me a big hug.

'I'm so sorry, Helen. I am sorry.'

I smiled, although I don't exactly know what the apology was for. Was she regretting her appalling behaviour at college over the last few months, or her behaviour at church, or her creating anxiety with the nights spent over at her boyfriend's place?

After work I texted Dex and offered to take him out for an early supper before his shift – my treat – so we went for a lamb pasanda. When the bill came, I realised I had forgotten I've currently got no card, and only had about 30p on me. Of course, the replacement cards have not come yet either, so Dex had to pay – even though it was meant to be me treating him! So embarrassing but I don't think he minded. I hope he didn't think I was taking advantage of his kind nature.

THURSDAY, JULY 15th

Hayley is getting even more strange, if that's possible. I was out on a call at the hospital this morning, but when I got back to the office Laura told me Hayley had been by, and looked a right state. 'She looked like she'd been up all night. Hair a mess, bleary-eyed, not making much sense at all. She came in and asked for the social worker on call, and absolutely insisted that in no way, under any circumstances, did she want to speak to you. The only person available was Maeve, and when she came out to see Hayley, she got a mouthful of abuse. Hayley told her not to bother, she'd changed her mind about needing to talk and everything was fine now, which obviously it isn't. And then she calmly turned round and walked out. She's an odd one.'

Thanks a lot, Hayley. After all I've done over the last couple of years for her, and now she decide she'll dump me and find someone else when she needs some help. I'm not going to be dropped so easily. I'm due to see her next week. Have to book something in for Wednesday, as have got another course on Monday and Tuesday. Hopefully everything is okay with her.

Felt sad tonight as I pondered Hayley not wanting to see me when she came into the office. Why has she suddenly turned against me – when only last week she was saying she was so sorry to me? Was she apologising in advance for giving me the elbow?

FRIDAY, JULY 17th

Good day at work. Justin, the lad with the hygiene issues, has at last been accepted into the placement that we've been working on. Went to say goodbye today, and was hoping for some warmth – and a sense that he'd washed recently. Got neither. Oh well, in this job, progress isn't always fast. Hope he'll be fine.

First rehearsal. Kristian did a good job, said that what matters is not our singing ability but the opportunity to get together, raise a vital issue and bring in some money to help Children on the Edge.

SUNDAY, JULY 18th

Hooray, hallelujah, and jolly good! We have a new leader! Sue spoke very powerfully this morning, husband Colin great too. Bizarrely, he could end up in the same staff room as Brian who teaches physics at Frenton Academy. Maybe they'll become good friends . . .

V is delighted too – and went up to Sue and apologised for not liking her before. This was very sweet, but might have been misguided sweetness on V's part. Sue had no idea about V's comments, she'd already left the meeting at that point. I wondered whether, rather than trying to be honest, it was necessary for V to say anything at all. She meant well, and watching them talking, Sue didn't seem to be fazed by it, so hopefully all is okay. Sue got a 92% vote, which is amazing. Hope the 8% who voted against will behave properly.

Phoned Robert and Nola to tell them the news. They're very pleased.

After church had lunch at Dex's aunt and uncle's place – they laid on an amazing feast. I can see why Dex was so aghast at my suggestion they were horrid. They don't resemble the Hemmings at all. Feel chastened about my obvious stereotyping of everyone who has a tendency towards legalism as mean and self-righteous. Brenda and Ron are throughly delightful. They obviously adore Dex; they've never been able to have any children of their own, but treat their Kiwi nephew like a son, and spoil him rotten.

MONDAY, JULY 19th

Interesting training course today about helping children of asylum seekers. Maeve was there, and kept asking questions she knew the answer to, so she could debate the answer with the course leader. Difficult people are not exclusive to the church.

Decided to go over to see Aaron again tomorrow night, I'm glad we've managed to stay friendly. Told Dex that Aaron and I were meeting up and he seemed perfectly fine about it, which is great, considering the fiasco in Marinabean. That's ancient history now.

TUESDAY, JULY 20th

I can't even begin to know where to start tonight. It's late – very late, but I'm hoping in writing this down, my head will at least begin to clear.

The balloon went up when I went over to see Aaron. He opened a bottle of wine, and I mentioned I'd been down to the police station to see if my purse had been handed in, and told him about the lovely surprise that some wonderfully honest person had done so. I was nattering about the hassle of cancelling my credit cards, and the embarrassment of forgetting I didn't have any and trying to treat Dex to a meal out.

'Getting my purse nicked has been a real pain. I've spent ages on the phone cancelling my credit cards, and even though they said I wasn't liable for anything that might have been charged in the couple of hours before I reported them missing, it was still worrying.'

'I know' he said, 'I remember when . . .' and then he suddenly trailed off. He stopped talking, and took another sip of his wine.

'You remember what?' I pressed. He shuffled in his seat.

'No . . . sorry to bring it up again . . . when I was attacked. I was too busy getting my head kicked in to notice one of the scumbags grabbed my wallet. There wasn't much cash in it, but my credit cards were. The police asked me not to cancel them for the first couple of days, in the hope one of the gang might be stupid enough to try and use them. But nothing happened, so in the end I had to make all those phone calls too . . .'

Something clicked in my head. I already *knew* Aaron had had his wallet taken, but who told me? 'Aaron, was there anything in the press about you being mugged? I seem to remember the newspaper said you were attacked. I don't think you've ever talked to me about having your wallet taken before.'

'The police didn't say anything publicly about my wallet being taken, because they wanted to give the impression they didn't know it was missing. I didn't say anything about it before because it wasn't important. What mattered terribly was what happened to your dad – me losing a few quid and my credit cards wasn't even worth mentioning.'

Call it a blinding flash of light if you like, or a terrible awakening moment, but I thought my heart was going to explode, it was beating so fast. The conversation I'd had with Hayley came flooding back into my memory: 'A life for a wallet with a few quid in it. Such a waste.'

I suddenly realised something that made me want to throw up. The only way Hayley could know Aaron had his wallet stolen was . . . *if she was there*. She'd even mentioned there wasn't much cash in it. The only way she could know that detail was if she had been involved in what happened.

I remembered her tearful parting shot the last day I saw her: 'I'm so sorry, Helen . . .' Suddenly it all made sense.

I burst into tears. The evil little cow. She must have been part of the gang who killed Dad.

I managed to blubber out what I'd figured out to Aaron, who asked where Hayley lived – I thought he was going to call the police for me. He didn't pick up the telephone, but instead said, very calmly, 'I'm going to get to the bottom of this, right now.' Then he grabbed his coat and ran out of the door.

I didn't know what to do. I didn't want to go chasing after him, and there was no way I was going to head towards Hayley's house. There's no telling what I might say or do to her. Nor did I want to call the police – what might that lead to? But I had to do something. What if Aaron decided vigilante justice was in order and tried to do something to her? Not that I could imagine him being violent, but he's always been unpredictable. But then again, did I care? She had lied to me, betrayed me, and all this time I had been running around like a gimp trying to help her. So that's what all her church visits were about – guilt. Or maybe she even got a sick buzz from being around the daughter of the man she'd been party to killing.

Decided to call Dex, and told him in about two breathless minutes what had happened and that Aaron was heading over to Hayley's house. Dex was great. He suggested he should follow Aaron, and intercept him before he got there. Then once he'd talked Aaron into letting the police take care of things, all three of us could go down to the police station and tell them the latest. It sounded like a great plan.

The plan failed. Aaron got there fast, ahead of Dex. Mrs Tennant opened the door, and when Aaron said he wanted to talk to Hayley about the death of Peter Sloane, started effing and blinding. Aaron reciprocated, so she called 999. Then Dex showed up, and tried to persuade Aaron to come away from the front door, and leave it to the police. Then Hayley came staggering down the stairs.

She was as high as a kite, apparently, and started shouting that she effing well had something she'd effing well like to show Aaron. She dashed back upstairs, and a moment later was waving a knife around in Aaron's face. 'There you go, clever boy', she screamed. 'That's all the proof you need. This is the knife that killed Helen's dad!'

Dex stepped forward and told her to chill out and put the knife down, but she started to wave it around some more, and somehow Aaron got between them and she managed to cut his arm. It was only a tiny nick, but Hayley freaked out and started sobbing between swearing and shouting she'd had nothing to do with the killing, which makes no sense at all.

That's when the police arrived, all sirens and blue flashing lights, and Mrs Tennant came out and shouted they should get Aaron and Dex off her property. But the police could see Hayley was high and dangerous. They arrested her for threatening behaviour, suspected use of illegal substances, and being in possession of a weapon. They took her away for questioning, took brief statements from Aaron and Dex, told Dex not to leave the country and let them go.

Aaron and Dex finally came back to the flat where I was sitting waiting, desperate to find out what had happened. Dex sat quietly while Aaron told me it all. Thank God Aaron wasn't badly hurt.

Dex took me home, and as we said goodnight, he asked if he could pray with me. And he did, a simple, heartfelt prayer. 'Jesus, give Helen peace, and a good night's sleep. Be close in this painful time, and help me to be helpful to her. Amen.'

Later

It was such a lovely prayer, but so far part of it hasn't worked, as it is now 3am.

WEDNESDAY, JULY 21st

The town is buzzing with the news of the arrest. Spent the evening with Mum. She is suddenly emotional over Hayley's arrest, it's as if this has given her permission to grieve some more. V, James and Laura came over tonight and talked and prayed with me. V didn't say much, but let me blabber on about my confused feelings about Hayley. I hate her, but after all these months and ups and downs, I can't stop caring about her. But she was part of the gang that killed Dad, and then she asked to come to church with me. Who knows – she may even be the killer. After all, she was waving that knife around.

Late tonight Nola called and we spent an hour talking it all through.

FRIDAY, JULY 23rd

Hayley didn't kill Dad, and she wasn't even there when it happened. But for the last few weeks or so, she knew who the killer was. The police stopped by my flat tonight. They came to tell me that Blag, Hayley's boyfriend, has been charged with murder.

When Hayley came down from her high, they started to question her. It turns out she was out on the town that night, but nowhere near the High Street. She was parked under the pier with one of her girlfriends, chain-smoking and swigging cheap whisky. The police had brought the other girl in for questioning and Hayley's alibi stacks up.

It seems that a couple of months ago, Hayley and a couple of her pals went for a day out to Duxford, and that's when she met Blag, who lives in a caravan park on the edge of the town. Turns out he's not her boyfriend in the conventional sense – that would be far too normal – but they started hanging out together and she spent some nights at his place. A couple of weeks ago they were both spending an evening getting out of their heads, and Hayley started talking about her appearance on the *Ross Daley Show*, and how Mike, one of the blokes she thought might have been her dad, had been so vile and abusive. Blag got angry and said he could hurt Mike for Hayley if she wanted him to. Hayley laughed in his face, said he wasn't that hard – he was all mouth and no action.

That's when Blag said he'd show her how hard he was, and started boasting about what happened in Frenton the night some old guy was murdered. Blag always carries a knife as a matter of course – insurance, he called it. He'd gone to Frenton with a gang of guys for a night on the juice, and were heading down the High Street in search of some fish and chips. That's when some skinny kid showed up (that would be Aaron) and they didn't like the look of him, and decided he could probably contribute some cash towards their chips.

Blag told Hayley there was some pushing and shoving, and then they all jumped the kid, put him on the ground, started to give him a good kicking, and grabbed his wallet too. That's when Dad showed up, yelled at them – and they turned on him. Somehow Dad had managed to put up a fight and had punched Blag in the mouth, and he'd pulled his knife and repeatedly stabbed Dad with it. The sick thing was that even though he was high when he told Hayley about it, he was very proud of himself. He'd even kept the knife as a souvenir rather than getting rid of the evidence. Obviously keen to prove how hard he is, Blag told Hayley he wasn't sorry about the old man dying, because no one punches him in the mouth and gets away with it. The only thing he was sorry about was that there was only a few quid in the wallet he'd lifted.

Hayley got scared and decided she wanted to go to the police, but then realised she had no proof. Blag would deny what he'd said and it would be her word against his. And so a few nights ago she'd spent the night over at his place, and while he was in the bathroom in the morning, she'd looked around his room – and found the knife in his bedside cabinet, together with one of Aaron's credit cards. Her plan was to take the knife to the police, but leave the card where it was so when they raided the place they'd find it and that would point to Blag.

Accordingly to Hayley, all this happened on Monday 12th. When the police told me this, I realised it was the very next day I had been to see Hayley, and she was acting so weirdly and going on endlessly about fathers. That's when she made the comment about the wallet – what Blag had told her must have still been fresh in her mind. She'd decided to go the police that day, but then made the mistake of watching the *Ross Daley Show* (that nauseating little man won't go away). Ross had spent ten minutes berating someone who had known about a serious crime, but hadn't immediately reported it to the police. Ross said that made his guest (or would that be his victim?) an accessory to the crime. That freaked Hayley out. Even though she had waited to gather some evidence to prove Blag was the killer, she had not gone right to the police. She realised she should have left it to them – they would have found the knife anyway, and the cards. Now she panicked that perhaps she was an accessory to murder. And that could get her into serious trouble.

She decided to think about it for a day or two, and then came up with the idea to talk to someone in confidence and find out her legal position. Hence her visit to Social Services, where she hoped to be able to talk to a social worker, but knew it couldn't be me. When Maeve came out to see her, she bottled it and headed out of the door.

She was drunk when Aaron and Dex showed up at her house. She said she's been so scared she's been hitting the bottle a lot. When Aaron said he wanted to ask her about Dad's death, she ran upstairs, got the knife and came running down to show them that she could prove who the killer was. But when they jumped back in fright, she realised she was a suspect. That freaked her out even more. Hence the erratic waving around of the blade and the minor cut Aaron got.

All of this came tumbling out in Hayley's interview – as soon as she sobered up, she was keen to tell the police everything she knew, whatever the consequences. The knife she'd been waving matches the description of the one used to stab Dad. A DNA test has proved it's definitely the one.

The police raided Blag's place; he was arrested and was brought in without a fight. The police picked up the credit card too. He's not so bold when he hasn't got a gang with him. They showed him the knife, and then he tried to say one of his mates in the gang did the stabbing, but they brought them in and the other three all said it was Blag. Then the police let him know they'd found Aaron's credit card in his place, and that's when he broke down.

Spent a long time on the phone talking with Dex, it feels like I keep going over the same things, but he listens patiently. I'm glad I have never met or seen Blag. It means I don't have a face to focus on with my hate filled thoughts.

SUNDAY, JULY 25th

Now I know who murdered my father, and so does everyone else in Frenton. Hayley is the talk of the town

– even a heroine. Because of her age the police tried to keep her identity quiet, but Mrs Tennant has been broadcasting the story about her niece being the brave soul who managed to blow the whistle on the Frenton murderer. The ghastly Mrs Tennant has even been asking if a reward is due.

People at church today were so kind. I struggled during communion, because I don't know where to begin in what to think about my attitude to Blag. He's been remanded without bail. I thought I would start to feel at least better, because at last now I know. But I still feel empty. I know who killed Dad – but he's still dead.

MONDAY, JULY 26th

Weird at work today. Obviously Hayley still has to have a link with a social worker, and under the present circumstances that cannot be me. It's been decided a social worker from another area will take her on. And so I handed over Hayley's case files to Maeve today, and I suddenly burst into tears. I'm not sure why. Much as I hated going to the Tennant household, it's odd to think I'll never be Hayley's social worker again. And she did risk her own neck to get justice for Dad.

TUESDAY, JULY 27th

Coffee with my mum tonight, who has been fantastic as usual. I don't know what to feel about Blag. He was drunk when he killed Dad. It's obvious this doesn't excuse him in any way, but it does mean he's not a cold-hearted killer who plotted to take someone's life.

He is is a thug and a bully – and now a murderer. God knows, he's probably going to have plenty of time to revisit his sins, although I do have a new worry – because he was drunk, this could end up being manslaughter, and then he could get off with a slap-on-the-hand sentence. Even trying to think this through makes me feel guilty. By even trying to understand the wretched Blag, even thinking about beginning a journey of forgiveness – it all seems as though I am betraying Dad. If I give Blag any benefit of any doubt, I feel like I'm siding with Blag against Dad – somehow making it a tiny bit acceptable that he stole his life away, which it isn't.

Would a new start be good for me? I don't want to leave Frenton, or NWCF – but I'm seriously wondering about a change of role in my job. Perhaps I could start working with the elderly? I feel I need to get away from here and all my memories, maybe take a holiday.

Dex has been wonderful. He listens, lets me cry, doesn't try to fix me or rush me through this. Aaron has been good too – he's texted a few times to make sure I'm doing okay. Glad, once again, we're still friends.

A glimmer of light: with Sue and Colin coming in a few weeks, perhaps there's a new season for NWCF. Hope so.

WEDNESDAY, JULY 28th

They tell me it's going to be at least three months before Blag's case can be heard. Have decided to try to file him away somewhere in the back of my head until the trial begins. Can't obsess over this every day. Hard discipline to do it though.

THURSDAY, JULY 29th

Trying to keep myself busy so I don't dwell over everything that has happened. Off work for a few days now, so repainted my sitting-room walls – an attempt at decorating therapy. After my meltdown over Hayley's file handover, I applied for compassionate leave, and although it took a couple of days to clear my desk, I'm glad for the space now. Finished the painting (off-lavender, very fresh-looking) and then set out to tidy the rest of the flat and generally get my life in some sort of order but ended up lying listlessly on the sofa flicking through day-time television.

FRIDAY, JULY 30th

Had an absolutely awful day over Blag today. I spent much of the day wanting to hurt him. I don't know how these things work, but it seems like today everything suddenly snapped into terrible focus and I could see a man's face laughing as Daddy died, half looking up at his sad loser hoodie friends for their sick approval. Felt such a rage I felt I should pray, so started pacing around the flat, initially praying, but then within seconds I found myself swearing loudly, over and over. Not even sure who I was swearing at.

FRIDAY, AUGUST 6th

I was walking down the Prom tonight, and suddenly round the corner came Hayley. I've been wanting to see her . . . needed to find the right moment. Tonight the right moment found me.

She stunned me by running up to me – she gave me a huge hug, and then started to cry.

I held her for a minute or two, and she let me.

'Hayley, I'm glad we've bumped into each other. Let's sit down for a while.'

We wandered wordlessly down the Prom. She was still sniffling and seemed to be struggling to speak. We found a seat, and for a minute or so we sat there, looking out to sea. There was so much I wanted to say, but felt I needed to allow her space to talk first. At last she did.

'Helen, it's probably nuts, but I feel rubbish that I ever hooked up with the bloke who killed your dad. Talk about a mad loser. I hate him. But at least it meant that, because of his big head and big mouth, I got to find out about what he did and helped him get what he's owed. I hope he's gonna be heading for a pension by the time he sees the light of day again.'

I looked at Hayley and realised once again she is a sad, lonely girl wanting someone to at least approve of her, never mind love her. I put my hand on hers. She didn't take it away.

'Hayley, you did a stupid and a brave thing. You continued to hang around a guy when you knew he was a killer. If he'd got wind you'd planned to report him, he might have killed you. But the police told me that, because of what you did, the case against Blag is cast iron, and so he's pleaded guilty. And I'll always – and I mean always – be grateful for that.'

Hayley's eyes filled up again, and she reached for a tissue, but now she was smiling too. But then her face clouded over.

'I've gotta ask you. That night when your bloke and the skinny kid – what's his name?'

'Aaron.'

'Yeah, them. That night they came round to our place. Did you think it was me who'd killed your dad? Do you think I could do that?'

I swallowed hard. 'I didn't know what to think. But when I realised you knew stuff about the murder which hadn't been released to the press, I suppose I did think you were involved somehow – maybe you'd been part of the group who did it. I don't know . . . it's just it seemed like the only explanation. And then when you kept

– 254 –

saying you were sorry, I jumped to conclusions. I've been doing that lately. I'm sorry. And, as I said, I'm thankful you took a big risk to help me and my family. It was crazy though.'

Hayley blew her nose, and then smiled again. She's got a lovely smile.

'Yeah, it was mad, but . . . I wanted to do something for you. I lost a dad, but then I never had a real dad in the first place – just a distant idiot who faked it by calling himself dad for a while and then shoved off when he felt like it. And then I got that mouthful from that scumbag Mike on the TV show. You had what I never had – a dad who loved you. I remember what everyone said about him at his memorial service – he sounded like a lovely bloke. And then he was snuffed out. I couldn't believe it when Blag told me he'd put the knife in. And so I thought I'd do my bit to help you to never have to wonder if your dad was gonna get some justice. I had to find the knife. And I did.'

She sniffed a bit more, and went on. 'For once, I actually managed to do something big. I hate him for what he did to your dad. And I am sorry about you losing him. I wish I'd met him.'

Now was my turn to cry.

We talked some more, and I explained why I couldn't be her social worker any more, because of the legal process with Blag.

'I get it, makes sense, I suppose. I hope I get someone who cares about me as much as you have. I know I've been a pain in the . . . well, a right pain sometimes. But . . . thanks. Thanks. Maybe I'll see you down at the youth centre sometime?'

I said I hoped so and explained I'm still not back there at the moment, but perhaps in the future. I desperately wanted to invite her to come back to NWCF, to give Alpha another try, but that's for her to choose without pressure from me. The last thing I'd want is her showing up at church just because she wants to please me.

And that was it. She got up to leave, said she was meeting some friends at the pier, gave me another hug and started to walk away. And then she stopped and turned around.

'Say a prayer for me sometime, will yer? I don't know about all this God stuff. I liked the Alpha thing, and even though I thought the pushy evangelist bloke who came to the church was a nutter, I still think there might be something in the Christian stuff. And I know God helped you when you lost your dad. Maybe he can help me now I know I never had a dad, and probably never will have one. So send one up for me, will yer?' And with that she was gone. I will send one up for her.

MONDAY, AUGUST 9th

Dex suggested I go back to work, which I did, today. Sitting around my flat wasn't doing anything to help me

– I focused on feeling angry and confused all day. Have also decided to get back into the rehearsals for the church music evening again, it gives me something to focus on. Another rehearsal tomorrow night.

TUESDAY, AUGUST 10th

The rehearsal turned out to be a lot more fun than I thought it would be, and a great distraction from all that's been happening over the last couple of weeks. It was pleasant to have a joke and a giggle with people at the church who were on the edge of physical violence with each other a few weeks ago. It's proof we do love one another.

The music evening is happening next Saturday evening, strangely, on Dad's birthday. Perhaps it's good I'll be so thoroughly distracted that day.

Brian called Robert and Nola and invited them down for the weekend, so they can enjoy the evening and see everybody. And they're coming! Hooray. Really want to be able to talk the Hayley/Blag thing through with them – hope they won't mind listening. Of course they won't.

SUNDAY, AUGUST 15th

Church was good. Seeing as Sue will be starting next Sunday, this is Brian's last weekend to lead the morning service. Dex came along too; I think it was mainly to give me some moral support, although he has said he thinks it might be good for him to come along to NWCF . . .

Met my mother for coffee in the poshest department store in Frenton and she paid. She's told me she's thinking about selling her home and moving to something a little smaller in the village. I initially froze: that was the house I grew up in! But she said it reminds her too much of Dad, and a new start might be good for her.

After thinking it through for a while I thought it might be a good idea. I love that house, but it's not the same without Dad. Why would I want my mum to suffer because I don't want things to change? (Well, some things anyway). I gave her a hug and told her that if that's what she wanted to do then she should go for it. She shed a tear and she said she didn't know how she'd managed to raise such a giving and beautiful daughter. Which made me tear up. So there we sat, hugging, crying and making a spectacle of ourselves. But we didn't care, some things are too important to be shy about. In some strange way Blag's arrest has enabled Mum and I to go deeper than ever before as we've talked about Dad in the past and her future.

Lord, thank you so much for having such a great mum. I pray that not a day goes by where you will not strengthen and bless our relationship. Amen.

Robert and Nola are back in town tomorrow. Hooray!

Great day at work – gave a fabulous presentation at an adoption hearing, even though I say so myself. The panel formally commended me for my work and approved my proposal. Have decided now is not the time for me to apply for a place on the panel . . . it would mean a lengthy conversation with Maeve.

After the presentation I went to see the adopting candidates and they cried buckets when I told them they had been approved. That's the amazing thing about my job; sometimes it feels like I am knee-deep in admin and boring procedures – and then there are times when I literally help to create a new family unit, like today. The intensity of preparing for the presentation has been good for me, too. I've been so distracted by it I only think about Blag about once an hour now – which is better than once a minute, so there's improvement.

Am missing seeing Hayley.

Tonight Robert and Nola stopped by. There were lots of hugs, tears, and we talked forever about Blag and the case and Warrington and how things are going for them. They seem very happy, but delighted to be back for a few days. So lovely to see them again. Listening to them talk with such enthusiasm about their new church plant, it's obvious they are in the right place. And although I never thought I'd say it, perhaps their moving on was good for NWCF after all. We've come through a lot of pain in the last few months, but I think we've learned some good lessons, and with Sue and Colin coming, I think we have some great days ahead. I hope so. Chatted on the phone for a while with Aaron tonight too. He's fine – says he's been seeing one of those giggling poetry girls lately. Hope it turns out well for him. Right now, am glad he's got somebody to hang out with.

WEDNESDAY, AUGUST 18th

Lovely coffee after work with Laura, Dex, V and James in Marinabean, and then on to the final rehearsal for the music evening.

THURSDAY, AUGUST 19th

Lovely lunch with V. I'm not sure if I'm right about this, but it seems marriage has changed her already. She is still the crazy for Jesus mad thing she's always been, but the madness is toned down. I think the terrible time we had in the church over the leadership selection, and the fact she's not proud of the way she handled herself in that mess – all of it has sobered her. And I've noticed she seems less keen to jump in with advice or even 'revelation.' We talked a lot about my feelings about Blag, and when I was expecting her to jump in with some scatty suggestion, she reached across the table and took my hand. I looked up and noticed a tear was running down her perfect cheek. 'Helen, I'm so very sorry, you've had to go through all of this. So sorry. I do love you, you know.' One thing's certain: I love V back.

Dinner with Dex and Robert and Nola, who all got along wonderfully: perfect, just perfect.

I did it after work, so no one could accuse me of doing personal business in work time. It felt strange parking my car outside Mrs Tennant's house, and I was not looking forward to stepping over her nicotine-tinged threshold again. But I needn't have worried. As soon as I opened the car door and got out, Hayley came bounding down the garden path, a huge grin on her face. Once again, I got the hug.

'Helen! So cool to see you. I got a visit from your boss today, she says I'm going to meet my new social worker next week, but in the meantime, if I have any stuff that needs sorting, I'm to contact her . . . she's a dull old bag, isn't she?'

I abandoned all professional etiquette and agreed that, yes indeed, Maeve is a dull old bag.

'So what's up? What are you doing here? Is everything okay? That scumbag Blag hasn't changed his guilty plea, has he? If he has, I'll testify, I'll do it. He's not going to get away with it.'

'No, he hasn't changed his plea. Everything's okay. But I wanted to stop by and give you something as a thank you. I don't know if you'll like it, but someone very dear to me once gave it to me, and I feel I want to pass it on to you. And no, in case you're wondering, it's not cash!'

Hayley laughed. I opened the car boot, and pulled out the print of Dali's pencil drawing of Peter.

'I want you to have this – you don't even need to put it on the wall if you don't want to – but keep it as a reminder.'

She took the print and stared at the image of the hot-headed fisherman. 'It's great. But a reminder of what?'

'This is a drawing of Peter, who was one of Jesus' best and closest friends. He was also loud, full of his own ideas, temperamental, and when it came to the crunch, he let Jesus down. But through all of that, Jesus loved him and trusted him, and turned his life into something beautiful. That didn't mean Peter had an easy ride, Hayley, but he was a bruised, messed up bloke who dis-covered Jesus would stick with him to the end.'

Hayley stared again at the picture, nodded, and then a frown formed on her face.

'And I suppose that's me, is it? Loud, prone to fly off the handle, likely to do the wrong thing . . . and you want me to know that, despite all that, God loves me?'

'It's not just you at all, Hayley . . . It's us. It's everyone. Me, you, everyone. Even Blag, although I'm not ready to think much about it yet. We've all got our stuff we're dealing with. We all make a hash of things, some more obviously than others. But all of us need to know we're not alone, we're not unloved or abandoned. Maybe it's hard to grasp, but none of us are the result of someone being a sperm donor who made us. Remember, back at Alpha, when you asked about whether or not God knows everything about you, and if he does, then does he still love you? Well, it's true. He loves us very much. Remember that, next time you feel like rubbish. And I'll try to remember it next time I feel like rubbish too.'

For the first time ever since I've known her, super-quick little Hayley was speechless. She stared at Peter for the longest time, maybe thirty seconds. Then she muttered, 'Thanks, Helen, thanks', kissed me on the cheek, and then crushed me into a goodbye hug. She smiled once more, tucked the picture under her arm, and walked back into the house.

Jesus, please let Hayley know how much you care about us all. Amen.

SATURDAY, AUGUST 21st

If I don't write this down now I think I'll burst. What a night, and I'm not just talking about the music evening. But first things first. I started the day by meeting Mum for breakfast. It being Dad's birthday, I thought we should be together, and we had an amazing time. She's got herself a new iPad and has imported loads of photographs into it, so we sat in Marinabean and flipped through their wedding photographs (stunningly ugly fashions from the seventies, amazing good looking and happy bride and groom). We cried some as we flipped through holiday snaps with us as a family looking so young and different. Then we took a walk down the Prom. Mum said she didn't think it would be a good idea to linger in the High Street today of all days.

Thought about Blag for a minute or two, and then decided I wasn't going to let him into this time with Mum and me.

Met Dex for quick coffee, and then spent a frantic afternoon at the church getting ready for the performance.

And so, to the music evening, which was a huge success. It was so simple, and that was the beauty of it. We sang a series of songs, all about God's heart for justice, there was a short DVD about Children on the Edge, and an offering. And again, not one song that was written by Kristian. I was so proud of him.

After all the heartache and arguments this year within NWCF, it was so nice to see everybody working together, having a great time, and all for a common cause. I can't believe that at some points I've thought about leaving this group of people, some of whom have been so supportive to me this year. Even when I've bailed out of attending church or been in a bad mood, some of them still continued to monitor me, phoning me up whether I liked it or not, and being kind to me. They've also pitched in with the youth club, a place I hope one day I can return to. Now Blag has been charged for the murder of my father, I feel like a lot of the stuff that was keeping me away from there has gone. Maybe I'll go back. Maybe not. We'll see. Would be nice to see Hayley there.

Brian stood up at the end of the music evening and thanked everyone for their hard work, and said what a fabulous example of teamwork and creativity it had all been. Then he said it was lovely to have Robert and Nola back for the weekend, and asked them both to come and say hello to us all, which they did. Nola cried when she said how much she missed us all: it was lovely to see them up at the front again; for a moment, things were as they were. Then Robert closed the evening in prayer, thanking God for the past, and asking for an even better future. We all said a very hearty *Amen*. Sue and Colin get 'installed' tomorrow – sounds like double glazing, but it will be a new era for NWCF.

And then a few of us went for supper *en masse* to a local pizza place, where we filled the table with pizza, pasta, salad and wine. Dex had come to see the music evening and was sitting beside me in the restaurant, being adorable. V and Laura were giving me knowing looks, and seemed to be generally nodding their heads in affirmation of my relationship with Dex. The S-Bs were there too – thankfully they had got a babysitter, so the meal was not disturbed by any infantile madness.

Mum asked for a moment to say something, and asked if we'd mind raising our glasses in honour of Dad, it being his birthday. We stood up, chinked our glasses, and Mum said, 'To you, Peter. Lovely man, much missed. Happy birthday.' Mum and I were tearful of course, but somehow it didn't cloud the atmosphere at the meal – in fact it seemed strangely right. Nola passed Mum a tissue over the table, and Robert gave Mum one of his enormous hugs.

After the dinner was over and we'd all tried to split the bill (a nightmare until Mr S-B stepped in and said he'd take care of paying it, his and Suzi S-B's treat, which was lovely) Dex suggested he and I go for a walk on the beach.

And it was then it happened. It was a clear, cold night, and I was cold so Dex hugged me closer to him. 'You know', he began. 'I don't think I've ever connected with anyone like you before. I feel like we go together, if you know what I mean? I know now that I love you, Helen Sloane. I love you. Do you think you could love me too? Do you think we have a serious future together . . . I suppose what I mean is . . . will you marry me?'

Here was a beautiful, sexy, normal Christian guy asking me to love him, to be with him always. A guy who loved God. A brilliant surfer. A guy who was not in any way related to the Hemmings. Oh my goodness. He was asking me to marry him.

I knew then, with absolute certainty, what my answer would be.

'Dex, I love you too. My answer is yes. That would be awesome.'

And it is.

Totally awesome.

The End

Children on the Edge

The musical at New Wave was to profile the work of *Children on the Edge*, a charity that exists to help the most marginalised and vulnerable children worldwide, those literally 'on the edge'.

The work of *Children on the Edge* brings hope, life, colour and fun into these children's lives. They are committed to ensuring their fundamental needs are met and rights realised. Their work throughout the world is guided by the UN Convention on the Rights of the Child, which guarantees every child the same inherent and universal rights.

From setting up safe play and education centres in post-conflict East Timor and post-Tsunami Indonesia, to preventing sex trafficking in Moldova, to working with children fleeing ethnic cleansing in Burma, COTE innovates and uses well proved practices in meeting children's social, emotional and educational needs, helping tackle and prevent the effects of disaster, conflict, loss and poverty.

Their aim is to give those who have been "robbed" of their innocence the childhood they deserve, because childhood should be a time of innocence and fun, exploration and learning.

For more information and to support their work, please go to
www.childrenontheedge.org